More Than Sexy

Sexy Series Book #1
Club TEN29

CARLY PHILLIPS

One protective alpha male plus one curvy damsel in distress equals an instant attraction they can't deny.

Billionaire nightclub owner Jason Dare doesn't stand a chance. From the moment he lays eyes on the luscious blonde stuck on the side of the road and realizes she's in danger, he goes from playboy to bodyguard.

Faith Lancaster's sweet body won't come to any harm on his watch. And watch Faith he does. He can't take his eyes off her. Jason will stop at nothing to keep Faith safe. Even if it means moving her into his apartment and letting her into his once private life.

Hiding from her past, Faith has spent the last year building her candy business into a profitable company while keeping to herself and staying under the radar … until she meets the delicious Mr. Dare. Alpha and irresistible, he awakens desires she has long denied. It doesn't take her long to succumb to his charms and fall hard for the man.

They both have their reasons for keeping things casual but when Faith's past catches up with her, can Jason finally claim the woman meant to be his?

Chapter One

WITH HAPPY HOUR being celebrated loudly around him, Jason Dare stood on a balcony above the bar area and surveyed his domain, Club TEN29, a nightclub in Tribeca, an ode to the past and a reminder that the future wasn't guaranteed. Despite the fact that his two partners were here, as were members of his actual family, he still felt very much alone.

Although solitary was a state of being he chose for reasons only he and his partners – men he considered his brothers – understood, sometimes it wasn't easy, especially since they were very much in demand. As owners, they were becoming well known here and had had extremely positive press, and that made him a target – for those who wanted an in with the occasional high-brow guest, and for women with dollar signs in their eyes and hopes to snag a wealthy man. Jason didn't engage. He was ultra-selective with the females he brought to his bed.

His life was the club, his partners, and his large

1

family. He kept his circle close and *minimized his risk of loss* as best he could. That mantra defined him, extending into his love life, as well. After his father had blown his family sky-high, after he'd almost lost his sister to cancer when she was a child, after losing his partner Landon's twin and Jason's best friend back in college, he didn't, couldn't get close to people and risk more loss.

He didn't get emotionally involved. Ever. A woman couldn't expect anything more than the occasional hookup when it was convenient, but he enjoyed those moments of connection with the females he did allow into his bed. He had enough darkness in his life that when he let go, he wanted to enjoy and have fun.

"Jason, this has been an amazing night!" his sister, Sienna, said, throwing her arms around his neck and planting a kiss on his cheek.

He chuckled and smiled at her glowing face.

Her husband, Ethan Knight, grinned as he pulled her off him and into his arms. "She's been liberal with the alcohol." Ethan explained her exuberant enthusiasm. "Her first time out since having the baby." He held his wife tight against him.

"I had fun! And now we're going home to f—" Ethan placed a hand over Sienna's mouth, sparing Jason from hearing about his sister's love life. Jesus.

He shot the man a grateful look.

"And on that note, we're leaving. We just wanted to say goodbye," Ethan said with a smug grin on his face.

"Thanks for coming." Jason extended his arm and shook Ethan's hand. "And give that little bundle a kiss from her uncle Jase."

Accepting this man as his sister's husband had been an adjustment, one Jason was still making, considering Ethan had knocked up Sienna before anyone even knew they were together. They now had a baby girl named Lizzy, who Jason adored, and Ethan was a member of the family. More people for Jason to worry about. He watched them leave, acknowledging his sister was in good hands with the other man.

His gaze turned to his closest friends since their time together in college, now equal partners in Club TEN29. They stood huddled together around the bar with some of their repeat customers. Tanner Grayson was the night manager, and Landon Bennett was the head of Entertainment and Appearances, Brand Deals, and Promotions. After Landon's twin died, he'd pulled into himself, while Tanner had spiraled, and it was only by sheer determination that he'd dragged himself out of the angry place he'd gone to and the trouble he'd gotten himself into.

Jason held the position of CEO. Together they were a solid mix of personalities and work ethic in a club that was merely two years old but becoming prominent in the night scene. They made sure Club TEN29 provided a memorable experience for everyone who stepped inside. There was no task too menial they wouldn't handle personally if the need arose.

But Jason wanted *more* for their singular club. They had a stage on which customers danced but it wasn't fully utilized, and although they'd put a lot of money into ads and promotions, they weren't growing as fast as he would like. He just hadn't figured out in which direction they needed to go in order to break out the way he wanted. Since Tanner and Landon thought things were fine as they were, Jason needed a fully fleshed-out plan before presenting it to them for a vote. Which was why he was meeting his cousin Gabe later on tonight. To hash out some ideas.

Gabriel Dare owned Elite, also a nightclub but one that operated on a scale Jason couldn't imagine, one where people paid over five figures for a table and A-list celebrities visited often. They had clubs all over the world, including on the island of Eden, an exclusive invitation-only resort near the Bermuda Triangle.

He wanted to think things through before he met up with Gabe, and he couldn't make decisions here, where the music blared and people partied. As much as Club TEN29 was home, Jason needed a break.

After clearing his departure with Tanner and Landon, Jason headed out into the cold air. He pulled his wool jacket around him and headed to his car. Despite it being impractical in the city, he liked having his Jag at his disposal.

Once he was enclosed in the luxurious interior and the heated seats and warmth began to surround him, he relaxed. He turned on some music and decided to drive around a little before heading to his cousin's. This area of the city wasn't the grid of ease that was Uptown Manhattan, and he wound his way through the smaller streets, taking in the shops that lined them.

Because it was cold, not many people were out, so when he came upon a lone van parked in front of a run-down apartment building, with two women standing alongside it, he slowed down. When one of the women bent over, her cute ass peeking out from beneath the edge of her down jacket, he noticed. And when she kicked what he realized was a flat tire in frustration, he came to a complete stop, then parked his car in front of hers.

As he climbed out and got a look at the curvy woman with waves of blonde hair, full lips, and a startled expression on her pretty face, currently clutching the lug wrench in her hand like a weapon, he realized his night was about to get much more interesting.

✧   ✧   ✧

FAITH LANCASTER LOADED the last of her marshmallow pops into the back of her company van, adjusting
the baskets, taking care to space the items far enough
apart that nothing would get ruined or crushed. She'd
spent all day in her small apartment kitchen, making
and wrapping her treats with the intention of dropping
off baskets to nearby stores along with her business
cards. She planned to request they leave them on the
counter for their customers to sample, hoping to drive
business to Sweet Treats, her candy store located off
the beaten path.

Kelsey Johnson, the culinary school intern Faith
had hired to help, joined her after working in the shop
all day. Before she and Faith could climb into the car,
Faith noticed her flat back tire and groaned.

The deflated tire mocked her and all the time she'd
spent creating and preparing. Although she could have
handed them out during the day, she'd ended up
spending all afternoon cooking and creating, deciding
to work from home instead of the shop, and now it
was early evening. But she knew the area she wanted
to hit up had open stores with people browsing for the
evening. A used bookstore, a coffee shop, and a few
other boutique-type stores that would hopefully help
out a fellow business.

She should have known better than to drop a big chunk of change on an old beat-up delivery van with no known history, but desperation made a woman do stupid things. And Faith, although she'd come a long way, had been desperate when she'd arrived in Manhattan with a new name, a limited amount of funds, and a dream of opening her own candy shop.

She glared at the flat on the back tire, wondering why luck just wasn't on her side. She'd had a rough go of it for a long time now, and she'd thought she was coming out on the other side at last. Now this.

"Kelsey, can you grab the lug wrench in the back? Just be careful not to knock over the candy. I'll deal with checking out the spare once I see if I can even get the lug nuts off." Assuming this old van even had a spare.

Kelsey, a pretty girl with brown hair and bangs, met Faith's gaze, eyes wide. "You can change a tire?" the twenty-one-year-old asked.

Faith managed a laugh or else she might cry in frustration. "I'm going to try."

When Faith was young, her dad, before abandoning Faith and her mother and older brother, had been a car fanatic. *Always have a lug wrench in your car, baby girl. It'll save you any time you have a flat.* Not that a ten-year-old knew anything about changing tires, but Faith had hung on her daddy's every word until one day he

7

hadn't come home. After that, Faith had given up on learning about cars, but she knew what she had to do from a class she'd taken in high school.

Accepting the lug wrench from Kelsey, she knelt down by the tire once more. When all her strength wouldn't turn the nut and she tried all four of them, she groaned, rose to her feet, and kicked at the tire in annoyance.

"Pretty sure that won't help," Kelsey said, just as Faith muttered an obscene curse thanks to the pain shooting through her foot.

She was in so much agony, she barely registered the car stopping, then pulling into the open spot in front of her van until a large man approached them, making her aware they were two women alone on an empty street in the dark.

Using the wrench as her defense, she held it up in front of her. "Don't come near us."

"Relax." He stepped to the side until he was underneath a streetlamp, the glow illuminating his features. "Do I look like a killer to you?"

She studied him, a handsome man with dark brown hair, in a wool coat with his tie visible. "Ted Bundy was handsome, too."

He grinned and her heart skipped a beat. My God, he was good-looking. A dimple beside that amazing smile winked at her, and body parts she'd thought long dead came to life.

"Thank you ... I think?" he said with a shake of his head. "Or not. Look, you obviously need help." He strode past her, ignoring her weaponry, and knelt down by the tire. "What about roadside assistance? Did you call?"

She glanced at his obviously expensive coat, had noted his suit beneath and brand name shoes. "Umm, does this old hunk of junk look like it comes with roadside assistance?" She shot him a look of disbelief. "Some of us can't afford luxuries and AAA is definitely a luxury."

From somewhere behind her, Kelsey, who had been silent, laughed out loud.

When he didn't immediately reply, Faith braced her hands on her hips and studied him, wondering why he'd stopped in the first place. "Listen, I appreciate the fact that you tried to help, but I'll figure something out."

He slowly rose to his feet. "Do you have a spare? You must if you were trying to take this one off."

"I assume I do, underneath all the baskets I just loaded into the back." She heard the frustration in her voice and fought back an inkling of defeat. She wasn't going to fall apart over a flat tire and ruined plans.

"You assume?" He shook his head and strode around to the back end of the van, glancing inside and muttering a curse.

"There's no obvious spare in here, so we'll have to unload all this to see what's underneath. What is all that anyway?" he asked.

"Candy. Homemade."

"Interesting." He raised his eyebrows, his gaze going from the sweet treats in the back to her face before he spoke. "Jason Dare," he said, extending his hand.

"Faith Lancaster." She placed her hand in his, and the heat of his skin sizzled against her palm.

"Nice to meet you, Faith." He curled his fingers around hers and lingered longer than was necessary for a handshake. Long enough for her body to tingle with awareness before he released her.

"And this is my intern, Kelsey," Faith said.

The other woman smiled at him but didn't shake his hand.

"What do you do for a living?" Faith asked in a husky voice she barely recognized, her entire body still hyperaware of that one brush of his skin.

"I own a nightclub. Club TEN29. Have you heard of it?" he asked.

She shook her head. She never went out to party at night, so what would she know about the club scene? But this man looked like he fit into it, with his sexy tousled brown hair that he probably paid a fortune to get cut so it fell just that way.

"Oh my God! My friends and I have been dying to go, but there's always such a long line to get in," Kelsey said, her excitement tangible.

She'd been so quiet, Faith had almost forgotten she was there.

"Well, here's my business card," Jason said, putting his hand in his coat pocket and coming out with a few cards. He handed one to Kelsey, who was bouncing on her feet in excitement. "Just show it to security and they'll let you right in or, at the very least, call me."

"Oh my God, thank you!" she practically squealed.

His gaze settled on Faith's face. "Now, let's see to that spare."

✧   ✧   ✧

IF JASON HAD to peg the type of woman he liked, tall and willowy would describe most of his hookups, yet he couldn't stop staring at the full-figured, curvy blonde with the porcelain skin and full lips who created candy, of all things.

"Let's move the baskets back to the apartment," Faith said, breaking the spell that had woven between them as they stared at one another, both clearly struck by something bigger than themselves.

"I'll take some." Kelsey walked between them and started to work.

Together they unloaded the candy, which Faith

and her assistant brought back upstairs to what he assumed was her apartment while he did something he hadn't done since college.

It was a miracle he knew how to change a tire.

For sure, his father, Robert Dare, hadn't taught him, as he'd rarely been around. Maybe he'd taught Jason's half brothers from a woman nobody knew about how to handle the things a man should know. Shaking off that painful memory, Jason called his cousin Gabe and let him know he would be late before throwing his jacket into the back of his car, rolling up his sleeves, loosening his tie, and getting down to his task.

While he worked, Kelsey called an Uber to take her home and one showed up quickly. Apparently Faith, having taken one of his business cards, had decided he was a legitimate businessman and safe to be alone with.

It didn't take long to get the tire off the van, and on examination, Jason realized it had been deliberately slashed, and that bothered him.

"How's it going?" Faith asked him.

"No problems, unless you count the fact that someone deliberately cut your tire." He glanced over his shoulder.

Faith had frozen in place, her eyes wide, her concerned expression clearly telling him she was upset.

"It's probably some of the kids in the neighborhood," she finally said, visibly forcing herself to relax. "They congregate around here late at night, and I haven't looked at the van since the day before yesterday."

He wasn't sure whether or not he believed her, and he tucked her reaction away to dissect another time.

She wrapped her arms around herself, appearing uncertain for the first time since he'd met her. And a fierce feeling of protectiveness rushed over him, one he'd previously experienced only for people he cared about, yet he didn't know this woman at all.

"So what are you doing with all the candy?" he asked as he worked on the tire, eager to take that stricken look off her face, change the subject, shake off the weird emotions she provoked in him, and maybe get to know her at the same time.

"I own a store called Sweet Treats," she said. "I want to build my business, so I made baskets of my signature item, and I was going to go around to the local businesses and ask if they'd put the candy and my business card by the register."

"What makes your candy stand out?" he asked.

"Other than how good it is?" she asked cheekily. "It's handcrafted and made with love. If I grow enough, I'll have to bring in outside-made candy to fill the cases, but that's for another time. Meanwhile, I know I'm a small shop and it'll be hard to get my name out there, but if I can dominate the area around my store based on the one thing I offer that's different than anyone else, then maybe word of mouth will work in my favor."

He listened to her words and his hand stilled on the last lug nut. Everything she said made sense.

Her words *dominating the area and standing out* jumped out at him. "That's it!" he said, excitement filling him because her words had hit on the one thing missing from Club TEN29. Something unique to them, and suddenly he knew just what he needed to discuss with Gabe.

"What's it?" she asked.

"You've come up with a brilliant idea, Faith Lancaster. And it just might help me with my business, so thank you." He turned the wrench one last time and rose to his feet, his legs stiff from crouching in one position for so long.

"Happy to help." She shrugged, obviously confused, but that was okay because he wasn't. He finally had direction.

He looked down at his hands, now completely covered in dirt and grease.

Faith glanced at his blackened skin. "Oh! Come upstairs and wash up. It's the least I can do for you after you saved me."

He didn't want to get into his car covered in filth, and she seemed okay with him now, so he nodded. "I'd appreciate that."

He followed her inside and up two flights of dark stairs. He immediately didn't like where she lived. From the description of the guys hanging out front late at night to the lack of lighting in the walk-up, it screamed danger. But who was he to judge? Yet it bothered him. He wouldn't let his sister live here.

By the time they walked into the small apartment, he was frowning, but one look at the cheerful décor and his mood lightened. This was a woman who made the best of any situation, he realized, taking in the white curtains and the old furniture with bright pink throw pillows covering the cushions. A matching fun pink rug sat under a beat-up coffee table covered in well-read books.

"You like pink," he mused, coming up beside her. "And candy." She even smelled sweet and delicious. "Are you fun, Faith?"

Her cheeks turned an adorable shade of ... pink. "I can be, in the right situation."

He wondered what that right situation might be, because he'd definitely like to have fun with her. The kind between the sheets. Before his dick could react to that thought, he asked, "Where's the bathroom?"

She led him to a small partly open door and gestured for him to go inside. "There's a tiny linen closet behind the door. Take a towel and get yourself cleaned up."

She stepped away and headed back to the main area of the apartment.

He glanced over to where the small kitchen was visible through a pass-through. The candies were neatly stacked on the Formica countertops.

"So about those treats. Did I earn myself one?" he asked, joining her.

She blinked in surprise. "Why didn't I think of that?" She rushed to the kitchen, returning with a pop and handing it to him.

He bit into it once, then twice, quickly swallowing the sweet, delicious candy. "Mmm. Damn, these are good. S'mores flavor?" he asked.

She nodded, a grin on her face. "It's like a taste of home," she said softly.

Sensing this meant something to her, he wanted to know more. "How so?"

She sighed. "My mom and I used to make candy all the time when I was growing up. She always wanted to open a store in our small town, but she didn't have the ability. Things were … out of her control. And she needed to work to take care of me and my brother. But this was her favorite recipe and it reminds me of her."

"What happened?" he asked. "If you want to talk about it."

"She died recently." Faith blinked and looked away.

Recognizing raw pain, he changed the subject. "Well, your candy is delicious and I hope you succeed," he said, treating her to a warm smile, realizing their time together was coming to an end.

"I have a meeting I need to get to," he said. But he wasn't ready to leave.

"Oh, right." She rushed over to the kitchen and returned with a basket in her hand. "Take this. As a thank you. You're a Good Samaritan, Jason Dare."

He accepted her gift, their skin brushing as it exchanged hands. A shot of electricity jolted up his arm and went straight to his cock. Something about this woman got to him, from her gorgeous face and curvaceous body to her strength and the hint of occasional fragility beneath. He knew with everything in him he ought to stay away. From the fact that her tire might have been slashed to the fact that she didn't radiate one-night-stand type of woman to him, he should say goodbye and walk out the door.

"Have dinner with me." He blurted out the words before he could think them through.

She stared at him in surprise, those pretty lips pursing in thought, green eyes huge. "Umm ... I really don't think it's a good idea. I have too much going on right now and I don't date and ... well, we shouldn't." She sounded sad, as if she didn't want to say no.

He rolled his shoulders, deciding it was for the best even if he didn't like being turned down by her. "I understand."

She stared at him for a heartbeat. "Well, thanks again."

He inclined his head. "You can thank me by locking your door and being careful out there." Her slashed tire stayed with him, bothered him, even.

Sure, this was New York City and not the best neighborhood, so it really could have been done by someone who considered vandalism a good time. He'd probably have gone with that theory, too, if not for her slightly panicked reaction she'd tried to hide.

"Don't worry. I'm a big girl and I can take care of myself," she said, striding toward the door. "But I'll take your advice."

He stepped out the door she'd opened for him. "Bye, sweetness," he said. "It was nice meeting you, Faith Lancaster."

She wrinkled her nose at the nickname.

"Would you prefer candy girl?" he asked, chuckling at the blush on her cheeks as he walked away.

✧　✧　✧

IF FAITH DATED anyone, she would date Jason Dare. She leaned back against the door and sighed like a teenage girl crushing on her first date. My God, that man had an ass to die for.

When she hadn't been carrying candy baskets upstairs, she'd been ogling his rear end in his suit trousers. She could only imagine him naked, and that was the idea that had her shivering when her thoughts should be on whether her slashed tire was a freak incident as she'd told Jason or a warning sign from the brother she'd run away from.

When they were younger, she'd loved her brother, but as he grew up, Colton developed ... issues and that was putting it mildly. Drugs took over his life.

She stepped away from the door, hating that she was going down this train of thought, but she couldn't help it. The tire had brought up all sorts of fears. And memories.

Colton showing up after her mom died unexpectedly, demanding his share of the estate, only to find out he'd been disinherited. His rage and anger. Though her mom hadn't been wealthy, she wasn't poor. She'd had money from her parents, which she'd saved, and she'd taken out a life insurance policy with Faith as the beneficiary.

She double-checked the lock and dead bolt on her door, as the memories continued to flow. As much as

Faith would have liked to share the money with her sibling, Faith agreed with her mom. Colton would throw the money away on drugs, so she honored her mother's wishes and refused him.

She should have known that wouldn't be the end of it. Colton came by high one night, broke into her apartment, grabbed her around the neck, and threatened to kill her. That was the moment she understood the brother she'd known was lost to her, and fear like she'd never known encompassed her.

Maybe she should have called the police, but she'd been afraid of angering him more. She knew from experience he never stayed behind bars for long, no matter what petty crime they picked him up for. So within three days of his threats, she'd quit her job, packed up the necessities, and left her small Midwestern town, heading to the biggest city she could think of, where she could get lost.

She'd checked into a hotel with cash, then found a lawyer willing to see her that same week, and he filed paperwork to change her name from Faith Holland to Faith Lancaster. Understanding the rush, he'd pulled strings to get her in to see a judge, who he convinced her life was in danger. And as she still had faint bruises on her neck, and photographs she'd taken immediately after, he'd been willing to seal her records.

She'd been in New York for a year and she'd

moved fast with everything she'd done. She had a new name, a new life, a shop she'd leased because it already had a commercial kitchen … and as she glanced around her apartment and out the window, she remembered she also had a slashed tire that might or might not present a problem.

Was it any wonder she'd turned Jason down? From the time her dad had left, leaving her to feel like it was her fault, that she was too much of a burden for him, she'd learned to distrust men. If the one who was supposed to love and take care of her couldn't stick around, why would someone she merely dated?

She wasn't a virgin, but she definitely didn't get involved with many guys. Yet for the first time, she'd been severely tempted to break her no-dating rule. Jason got her blood pumping, desire flowing, and he made her want to step out of the hidden comfort zone she'd cushioned herself in for most of her life.

But she couldn't. She knew better than to trust any guy, let alone a nightclub owner she'd just met. Even if he had been her savior tonight.

Chapter Two

J ASON DROVE AWAY from Faith's apartment, a basket of candy on his passenger seat and his mind on the sexy woman he'd left behind, an unusual occurrence. He never had problems leaving a female in his rearview mirror. He wasn't an ass, he just didn't get attached. Something about Faith got to him, and considering she'd turned down his request for a date, he'd be better off forgetting about her. Except her tire had been slashed…

He shook his head and rode uptown to his cousin Gabe's apartment. His wife, Izzy, greeted him at the door, her three-year-old-son, Noah, in her arms, her wild hair a halo around her head, her pretty face lighting up at the sight of him.

"Jason! Come on in. Gabe said you'd be stopping by."

He kissed her on the cheek and chucked the boy under the chin. "Hey, little man. You're getting so big."

The child held up three fingers, wiggling to get

down from his mother's grasp. "I was just going to give him a bath. I'll get Gabe for you," she said.

As he stepped into the apartment, Gabe met up with him in the entryway. He paused to play with his son, lifting the child into the air and laughing with him before settling him into his mother's arms, and they headed for his bath.

"I'm always shocked to see you so light-hearted and laughing," Jason said. "Sorry. It's just so different from the man you were."

Gabe's eyes lit with pleasure. "Look what I have in my life to make me smile." He glanced toward where Isabelle had taken his son. "You'll see yourself one day."

"Oh, no," Jason automatically said. "My life is full enough."

"Until you meet the right woman."

Jason's thoughts immediately went to the gorgeous, shapely blonde with a good sense of humor and the ability to charm him. "Hey, I brought you some candy," he said to Gabe, lifting the basket. "A … friend gave it to me."

"Is this *friend* the reason you're running late?" Gabe asked, a wry smile on his face.

Jason winced. "She ran into tire trouble." He didn't mention that he'd just met Faith when he saw her on the side of the street kicking her van. He recalled that moment with an amused smile.

"I'll take that grin as a yes. So who is she?"

Jason chuckled, then decided to confide in his cousin, after all. "I met her tonight. She had some issues and I helped out. She has a candy shop near the club."

"So you decided to be a Good Samaritan."

He nodded.

"And she thanked you with treats. That you like, a lot."

Jason rolled his eyes. "Can we discuss business?"

Grinning, Gabe gestured into the apartment, and Jason followed him through the huge open design and into his private office, where they settled into wing-back chairs. "Drink?" Gabe offered.

Jason shook his head. He wasn't a big drinker. Not since that night. "No, thank you."

"So what's going on?" Gabe had been Jason's mentor since he'd finished college and decided to stay in New York with his now-partners. He'd helped him find an apartment and funded his venture, Club TEN29, named after the date Levi died. A date the men would never forget.

"Now what did you want to discuss about the future of your club?" Gabe leaned back in his chair and met Jason's gaze.

"I came here to ask for ideas, but when I was talking to Faith earlier…"

"The candy girl?"

Jason laughed. "Yes. She mentioned wanting to stand out in her area of business and dominate, and I realized that's what we needed to do and an idea came to me on how. We should expand Club TEN29, utilize our stage, and upgrade our acoustics. Then we bring in live talent. I want a Miami vibe in New York." His excitement grew as he explained. "I don't expect big names off the bat, but I know we can get solid people. I can hit up Avery's husband, the rock star, for help." Jason had also dated Charlotte Jasper, another recording artist he'd met through his half brother-in-law. He could ask her to perform.

"All of which would require funding." Gabe steepled his fingers in thought.

Jason nodded. Gabe had his hands in various businesses and had the money to lend should he deem it a worthwhile investment.

"We have the collateral now to go to a bank for a loan." Which they hadn't had when they were starting out. Gabe had lent them the money for the start-up, which they were still paying back over time. "But I'd prefer to work directly with you again."

"Talk to your partners and see if they're on board. Work up a plan and bring it to me."

Jason rose to his feet. "Thank you."

Gabe stood, walked over, and slapped him on the back. "Your success is my success. Besides, we're family."

Their grandfathers had been brothers but the Dares remained close despite some living in different states. Even the half-siblings had come to an understanding and had sibling-like relationships now. Some more than others.

"Enjoy your family," Jason said to Gabe as they walked to the door.

"Thanks. Enjoy your candy girl."

Jason's heart gave a kick. "I don't think I'll be seeing her again." She'd made it clear she didn't think it was a good idea, and if he had to look deep into his soul, the part of him he protected, he had to agree.

But he still couldn't forget the slashed tire or the troubled look that had crossed her face when he told her about it.

"Letting her go easily doesn't sound like the Dare way," Gabe said before saying goodbye and shutting the door.

Jason groaned and headed back to his car, Gabe's words in his ear.

✧   ✧   ✧

AFTER HER FAILED attempt to deliver candy and meeting her dark knight, as she'd come to think of

Jason Dare, Faith spent a restless night tossing and turning. She had too much on her mind to relax. From the need to reschedule her candies to a daytime delivery, which meant taking time away from being in the store, to her worry about Colton finding her, to thoughts of the sexy man she'd turned away, she was unsettled, to say the least.

She woke up extra early and made herself a cup of coffee in the Keurig she'd splurged on, poured in some cream, and grabbed a cup of yogurt. No Greek yogurt for her; she liked the tiramisu-flavored kind, sugared and all.

She settled in at the kitchen island that doubled as her table and powered up her laptop. With Jason's card beside her on the counter, she pulled up the website for Club TEN29, telling herself it was mere curiosity overall that compelled her. That she wasn't cyberstalking Jason Dare.

At a glance, she was impressed with the interactive website and the wealth of information and rooms available on the premises for events and parties. The website provided music and gave a much more professional impression than the basic site she'd created for Sweet Treats.

Professional website, she jotted down in the notes section of her computer. Another expensive item on her to-do list for her business, she thought with a sigh.

Then, unable to help herself, she clicked on the *About* section, and photographs of the three partners came up in full color. Jason had the lightest brown hair, the other two men were darker, all sporting a scruff of beard, but it was Jason's startling indigo blue eyes that stood out. If she hadn't been so over-whelmed, she'd have paid more attention to them last night. She studied him, his intense gaze, slightly brooding, sexy look, and sighed, squirming in her seat at the sight of him.

Scrolling further, she came to the meaning of Club TEN29 and sucked in a startled breath. The words were brief but impactful: *Club TEN29 is named in memory of Levi Bennett, who died in a tragic accident on October 29, 2009,* beneath the photograph of a young man who appeared almost identical to the older photo of Landon Bennett. They must have been twins. How tragic and sad, she thought, closing out of the website.

But not before taking one last lingering look at Jason and feeling a sense of regret for what might have been if her situation had been different and she'd been free to see him again.

She made a note to go to a gas station and order a new tire for her old van and get the others checked before turning her attention to ordering supplies for her shop. Incoming orders were coming in surprisingly quickly, and she was thrilled with her slow but steady growth and return clientele.

After she finished her *paperwork*, she showered and dressed in dark jeans and a sweater, pulling on her lightweight puffer jacket for the day, and loaded up her van again with her candy. She stopped to open the shop for Kelsey. While her intern handled sales, Faith would drop the baskets off at various local businesses. If she didn't do it today, the candy would start to go stale, and she didn't want anything to go to waste. She was operating in the black by being careful.

She spent the day working, and though she wished she could say she'd put Jason Dare out of her mind, she couldn't stop thinking about him, his tight ass, and the warmth in his eyes when he looked at her. But she reminded herself that he didn't need trouble in his life and that's what she was running from. Trouble in the form of her brother.

✧　✧　✧

JASON HAD TEXTED his partners, telling them he wanted to meet in the morning at the club, which was why he was walking upstairs inside the darkened venue at noon the next day. The guys had been up late, so Jason had pushed the time to a more reasonable one. If it had been up to him, he'd have been here by nine.

He joined them in the large space they occupied as their shared office, when they weren't holed up in their individual private rooms, to find the guys in jeans and tee shirts, both Landon and Tanner guzzling coffee and glaring at him.

"This had better be worth dragging me out of bed," Tanner muttered. "I'm fucking beat."

Landon yawned. "What he said."

Jason wasn't surprised. Landon was a man of few words.

Jason flipped on the overhead lights, guaranteeing his friends perked up. He waited for the cursing and groaning to end before he gestured through the window that overlooked the main staging area below.

"Imagine an A-list artist performing on stage. Now picture the lines to get in. A Miami vibe in New York. A whole new TEN29." He gave his pitch, short and sweet. "So much stronger than *come on in and dance*," he added for good measure.

When the two men looked at him over their coffee cups, he frowned and went on. "We started this club and built it into a respectable business. I want more. We're capable of being *more*. In honor of Levi, this place should be *more*."

Their eyes narrowed at the mention of their friend, Landon's brother, who'd died too young. In a stupid way, because they'd all been too afraid to walk away from a situation they'd committed to and didn't know how to get out of. They all blamed themselves, yet none of them blamed each other.

Was Jason challenging them to step up? Hell yes. "We don't want to get complacent," he said.

"I'm in," Landon immediately said, the mention of his twin clearly getting his juices flowing.

Jason wondered if he could convince his talented friend to play the guitar on stage. Not something he'd bring up now. It was too early in the process, and Landon had avoided his instruments for years because he'd used to play with his twin.

Right now, Jason just needed them on board for the change of direction in the club.

Glancing at Tanner, Jason waited.

"Yeah. You got my vote," Tanner finally said. "We need to build and find our own niche. Get away from the other basic clubs and the best way is to outclass and outsmart them."

"Not play dirty the way some of them do," Jason said, glancing at Tanner, whose temper was legendary, trying to remind him, by sheer force of will, he needed to continue his good behavior and stay out of trouble.

Tanner got the message, lifting his hands in a gesture of peace. "No worries here."

They all hoped Tanner was finished using his fists to make his point. Ever since going into business, he'd thrown his energy into the club and channeled his anger into positive pursuits.

"So we need a plan," Jason said. "Money to bring in the acts. Landon, booking is your specialty, but I'd like to talk to my brother-in-law. See if Grey Kingston will perform for us or talk us up to other musicians." He didn't mention Charlotte yet.

Bringing her into the mix was risky because she'd wanted more than Jason had been willing to give. If he asked her to come to New York now, she might take it as a sign he'd changed his mind about a relationship. He hadn't.

Not with her.

Not with anyone but... He still couldn't get a certain curvy blonde out of his mind.

He glanced at his friends. "It's that easy? You're both in agreement that this is the direction we should go?"

Landon shrugged. "I like the concept. What did Gabe say?"

"To talk to the two of you, then bring him a viable plan."

Landon walked over to the window and stared out at the empty club. "I'll bring in an expert on live-act PA systems. Get an estimate on upgrading not just the equipment but the acoustics. I'll also make a list of possible acts."

Tanner nodded. "And I'll put together an estimate to make sure our security systems are upgraded to the best ones available. If we're having top talent, we need to take security seriously."

With their support, the worry inside Jason eased. He should have known better than to think his *brothers* wouldn't agree with his ideas for making the club even better.

His cell rang and he pulled it from his pocket. "Gabe?" he asked as he took the call.

"No. It's Izzy on Gabe's phone. Where did you get that basket of candy you left? Oh my God, Jason, it's delicious!"

He wished he hadn't brought them the candy and had kept it for himself. Hell, any reminder of Faith would have made him happy, but he was glad Izzy had enjoyed. "I met a woman who owns a shop called Sweet Treats. Her name is Faith Lancaster."

"I want them as part of the giveaways at Noah's birthday party. Can you get me in touch with the owner?"

An excuse to see Faith again? The ability to help her grow her business? He held back the fist pump, but his heart began a rapid beat inside his chest. Clearly he couldn't get this woman out of his system by trying to forget about her, so he was going to have to find another way to cure his craving.

Seeing her again would be a start. "I'll talk to her and have her give you a call," he said to Gabe's wife.

"I'd appreciate it. This woman has talent," Izzy said. "My friends are going to be so jealous I found her first." She laughed at the thought.

He shook his head and grinned. He'd always liked Gabe's woman. "I'll get in touch with her for you."

"Thanks, Jase. You're the best." She disconnected the call and he hung up, sliding his phone back into his jeans pocket.

"What's with the shit-eating grin on your face?" Tanner asked.

"And who's the *she* who put it there?" Landon asked as a follow-up.

Jason groaned. He'd never been able to keep anything from these guys. As far back as college, from the time they'd met, the four of them, Levi included, had been tight. And if Levi hadn't insisted on them joining a damned fraternity... He shook his head, pushing those thoughts from his mind. That was the only way he could live with the pain. Shove it away hard.

"I met a woman the other night when I left the club to see Gabe. She had a flat tire on an old beat-up delivery van she was using and I stopped to help."

"You changed a tire? In your Ferragamo shoes and Canali suit?"

"Damned right I did and don't look so surprised. I can get my hands dirty once in a while." Especially for a gorgeous woman like Faith.

With a renewed sense of purpose, Jason turned to his friends. "So everyone has their assignments? I've got somewhere to be."

"We're on it. Go get laid," Tanner said with a chuckle.

He wished. "It's not like that with this woman."

"Oh, fuck. So it's like *that*?" Landon shook his head. "If you aren't interested in fucking her–"

"I didn't say I wasn't. Just that I'm staying away." Because she didn't think them dating was a good idea and he'd agreed. Jason started for the door, done with this conversation.

But apparently his friends weren't. "Not taking her home and fucking her means you're worried you could get serious about her," Tanner said, sounding almost gleeful. If he could get under someone's skin, it made Tanner happy.

"Shows what you know." Jason threw the words over his shoulder as he walked out, but he was very much afraid they were right.

Faith Lancaster was in his head and he was beginning to think the only way to get her out was to see what, if anything, could be between them. And now, luckily for him, he had an excuse to see her again.

✧　✧　✧

FAITH WOKE UP and performed her usual routine,

36

settling in for her cup of morning coffee and a look at her website, orders, and sales numbers. Right now it appeared that her online orders had picked up and in-store sales were strong. Her goal with the baskets had been to increase both of those as well as her foot traffic, and a click would tell her if she'd had initial gains.

She clicked and ... "Success!" There had been an exponential jump in the three short days since she'd left her baskets in stores downtown. It felt good to accomplish her goal, better to know her ideas had merit and were working for her.

She wondered if whatever notion she'd given Jason Dare the other night had helped him the way he'd hoped it would. She'd picked up his business card a few times over the last couple of days, wishing her life was simple and that she could call him. At the very least to just be his friend. But it seemed like lying low was working for her.

Things had been quiet since the tire slashing, leading her to believe it had been a freak incident. Maybe one of the neighborhood kids really had thought vandalism made for a fun night out. She couldn't afford to bring anyone into her life that might bring attention to her or become a target her brother could use against her.

If she was lonely, well, at least she was safe. It was

a trade-off she was willing to make.

After getting dressed, she headed out for the day, still on a high from the results of her experiment for her business. But when she pulled up to the front of the shop, her world fell apart. Graffiti covered the glass, ruining the beautiful painting she'd had done of her logo, and the glass on the door had been shattered.

She parked and walked to the entrance, her stomach twisted in painful knots, and tears sprung to her eyes. She hadn't been able to afford a burglar alarm and because she was surrounded by so many other stores, she'd naively thought she could get by without one.

The shops surrounding her were clothing stores whose salespeople didn't arrive for work until ten a.m. She came in early to prep and cook. Obviously no one had reported this yet or the police would be here.

With her heart in her throat, she dialed 911 and stood outside before entering, only willing to do so with a police officer by her side. While she waited, she'd never felt so alone or experienced the solitude of her life more acutely. She'd left behind a life with friends, who she hadn't contacted for fear Colton would pressure them for her whereabouts.

And though she had Kelsey here, Kelsey was an intern, not a real friend. At twenty-five, Faith was four years older than the other girl, who had her own group

of friends from school. New York City wasn't condu-
cive to meeting people if you didn't make an effort, go
to the gym or classes, and put yourself out there. And
Faith had done everything but. She'd kept her head
down, run her business, and gone home alone at night.

Her thoughts went to Jason, a man she'd just met.
She felt silly, but she'd put his business card in her
jacket pocket, and she fingered the cool paper now,
hoping it would make her feel better, but she had no
intention of calling him.

He didn't need her problems and he wasn't her
friend. He'd just been a helpful stranger.

She forced herself to think about the incident and
who could have done it. If her brother had been the
culprit, and how could it be anyone but him, how had
he found her? She'd put all the paperwork in the
business entity name, not her own, hadn't put her
picture on any of her social media, including the
company website, and she'd taken a new last name to
ensure she'd be protected. But if these two back-to-
back episodes told her anything, there was no such
thing as safe.

Once the cops came, they checked out the business before declaring it clear for her to go inside, at
which point she had to step over a brick that had been
thrown through the glass. Thank God whoever it was
hadn't gotten inside. Her equipment and cases were all

intact and she blew out a relieved breath.

A forensic analyst arrived to dust for prints and bag the brick for evidence, while another officer took Faith's statement. She debated telling them about Colton's attack and threats, but that could only lead to them contacting the police department at home to question him, and she didn't want to alert him to where she was on the very off chance this was a coincidence. If they found his prints, they'd have proof. He had a record, after all. But if they didn't, they couldn't accuse him anyway.

Finally they left her alone with the mess of her shop. Luckily for her, the man who owned the clothing store on one side came by and called a few friends, who boarded up the door until she could get someone in to fix it during the week. And there was nothing she could do about the graffiti until the window washers could fit her in.

She refused to let her brother frighten her out of her own shop, so despite the boarded window and mess outside, she prepared her candy for the day and opened for business.

✧　✧　✧

THREE DAYS PASSED before Jason was able to give his undivided attention to Faith. He didn't want to approach her with something heavy on his mind, and with his mother's divorce going on in Florida, her sudden spate of phone calls to Jason, his brother Alex's follow-ups, and Sienna's added distress, combined with the business issues, Jason had had his hands full. When he saw Faith again, he wanted to be wholly focused on more than just asking her to contact Izzy about Noah's birthday party favors.

He wanted a game plan about *them*.

Gabe's comment about Jason's actions when it came to Faith stayed with him. *Letting her go easily doesn't sound like the Dare way.* Jason was well aware that Gabe had waited a long time for Izzy, and when he'd finally gotten his chance, he'd had to let her go find herself before she could truly become his. However, Gabe had kept a silent eye on her the entire time.

With Faith's face and sexy body in his dreams and firmly entrenched in his mind, Jason had been fighting his instinct not to get involved when everything inside him screamed out for him to check on her. See her again. Make sure the tire was a fluke and she was safe and okay. Now, he finally had a reason to seek her out, and he'd decided to push harder to see what could be between them.

He might not want to add someone else to the list of people he had to worry about, but in one short night, she'd gotten under his skin, giving him no choice.

He headed for his car and typed her store name into Waze, ready to put his plan into motion. Except when he approached the shop, located on the left, as his direction-voice told him, he saw graffiti covering the windows and the door to her store boarded up.

"Fuck." Stomach churning, protective instincts growing inside him, he drove around, searching for a parking spot, finally settling on a lot a few blocks away. He gave his car to an attendant and rushed down the street and over to Sweet Treats.

He opened the door, which still worked, and stepped inside. The sweet smell immediately assaulted him, a delicious, welcoming scent that reminded him of his candy girl. Inside, there was no hint of vandalism, thank goodness, but he didn't see Faith.

"Hello?" he called out.

She immediately popped up from where she must have been kneeling down by the counter. "Jason!" she said, obviously surprised to see him.

"What the hell happened here?" he asked, knowing he sounded pissed because he was. Who would terrorize a woman this way?

She sighed. "The store was vandalized on Sunday and nobody's been willing to come out and fix it until sometime next week."

"Sunday? Why the hell didn't you call me?" Guilt for ignoring his gut instinct immediately filled him.

Hadn't he worried about the slashed tire? Didn't he know better than to disregard what his instinct told him was important? He tamped down on thoughts of Levi. Faith was here in front of him, safe at least right now, and he intended to make sure she stayed that way.

"Seriously?" She strode out from behind the counter, hands settled on her hips, and glared at him. "I barely know you. Why would I bother you with my problems?"

He stepped closer, placing his hand beneath her chin, their gazes locked in a war of wills. "Because there was a connection between us and you know it. And because I can help you and clearly" – he swept his arm toward the door – "you need that help and support. Where is Kelsey?" he asked more gently, stroking a hand over Faith's cheek before stepping back and giving her space.

Faith let out a breathy groan. "She's out with the flu. I've been holding things down here alone, but like I said, people aren't coming in. I think they're avoiding me because of the graffiti and damage." She frowned, appearing more angry than scared, for which he was grateful.

He took her soft hand in his and looked her over, inspecting her body, from her feet in pink Chucks, up her legs, past her apron, over her abundant and tempting breasts, to her hair piled on top of her head. "You look fine," he muttered to himself, relieved.

She blinked in clear disbelief. "Now that's a good way to turn a lady's head. *You look fine,*" she said in a damned good imitation of him.

He shook his head and grinned. "I meant, you appear unharmed and you look fucking fantastic." And she did. The messy bun and hot pink tee shirt with her store logo hugging her curves suited her.

She laughed. "Now you're just sugarcoating the truth."

"And you're trying to avoid discussing what happened here." He pulled her over to the nearest table and held out a chair. "Sit and talk to me."

She narrowed her gaze as she lowered herself into the chair. "I came in early on Sunday and found … this." She gestured to the window, her expression alternatively sad, then furious.

He slid his chair closer to hers before settling in. "Do you think it's related to the slashed tire?"

"I have no idea," she said, as her entire expression suddenly shut down.

It hadn't been his imagination, either. One minute she'd been engaged in the conversation; the next she'd closed herself off to him.

From the minute he'd laid eyes on her, he'd marked her as special. He still wouldn't let himself think of her as his. She was right in saying they barely knew each other. But if she thought he was going to let her get away with deflecting about something as important as her safety, she was about to learn that Jason Dare didn't screw around when it came to people he cared about. And she'd just been added to that short list.

Chapter Three

J ASON UNDERSTOOD WHEN to tread carefully, so he studied the suddenly panicked look on Faith's face and decided to tackle things from another direction.

"Okay you obviously don't trust me … yet. So let's start this way. I'm going to get your business back up and running." He'd prove to her she could believe in him and he wouldn't let her down.

She frowned, shaking her head. "I called everyone in the area and some beyond. People are booked up."

He raised an eyebrow at the challenge and pulled out his cell, dialing one of his contractors who'd done work at Club TEN29 and who owed him a favor.

"Sam? It's Jason Dare."

"Hey, man. How are you?" Sam Fremont asked.

"I'm okay. You? How are Lisa and that princess of yours?" he asked of the man's daughter.

"Doing well. The doctors say just two treatments left," he said, his relief obvious in his voice.

"Good! Listen, I'm sorry for the short notice, but I have a friend with an issue." He went on to explain about Faith's graffiti and the glass on the door. "How soon can you get someone out here to fix both?"

Sam had access to glass cutters, window cleaners, and anything else Faith might need.

"I'll come over myself to assess the situation and handle what I can. What I can't, I'll call in reinforcements to fix. Be there in an hour. Just text me the address."

"Great. I owe you one. I'll be here to meet you in an hour," he repeated for Faith's benefit, whose eyes opened wide.

"How did you do that?" she asked, as he typed her address and store name into his phone for Sam.

He didn't find it easy to talk about this, but it was a step toward building trust, and if he was going to keep her safe, he needed to understand what she was up against. It was more than neighborhood kids. That much he knew.

He cleared his throat and looked into her pretty green eyes. "Sam's daughter was diagnosed with childhood leukemia and he panicked. He was a freaking mess."

"I can't even imagine," she said, her heart in her voice.

"Well, my sister lived through it when she was young. She had a bone marrow transplant." The necessity had led Jason's two-timing father to reveal to his wife that he needed to have his full siblings tested to see if they were a match. Their lives had all blown up at the time.

"Jason, I'm so sorry." Faith reached out and held his hand. "How is she?"

"Fine now. Healthy. A mom." He grinned at that. "But I got her in touch with Sam and his wife, Lisa. She talked them through the process, kept them calm, reassured them when she could." He shrugged. "Sam feels like he owes me."

He shook his head, and when things came back into focus, he realized Faith had tears in her eyes.

"You have a big heart," she murmured.

"It just made sense," he said, uncomfortable with the praise for something so minor. "Sienna went through the same experience and I knew she could help them. And now Sam will help you. This place will be back to itself in no time."

"I don't know how to thank you," she murmured.

"I do. Go on a date with me," he said, back to his pushy, what he hoped was charming, self. Was he playing fair? No. did he care?

Not one bit.

He started to rise before she could answer him, deciding that he'd effectively backed her into doing something she wanted to do anyway.

"Jason—" she said, warning him with her tone she

didn't like being pushed into a corner.

"I know. It's not a good idea." He met her gaze. "I'm just waiting for you to explain why the hell not?"

"Fine. Sit back down."

He did as she said and waited patiently, understanding whatever she had to explain was obviously difficult for her.

"My mom passed away without warning a little over a year ago." Tears filled her eyes and he reached out, clasping her hand in his.

"I'm sorry."

She sniffed. "Thank you. Me, too. Anyway, I lived in Iowa, where I grew up. My dad left when I was almost eleven. I have no idea what happened to him, but Mom somehow made it okay. She worked to make ends meet, and I went to a local college, worked in a store in town. It was my brother who was the problem. He acted out after Dad left, and eventually he was doing drugs, selling with a local dealer. Mom threw him out."

He listened, sad for the little girl who'd lost her dad and whose brother hadn't manned up. "What happened?"

"After Mom died, Colton showed up, demanding his share of the inheritance. There wasn't much, but Mom had saved money from her parents, and she'd taken out a life insurance policy. Everything went to me."

"She disinherited him," Jason said and Faith nodded.

"She had no choice. He would have spent it all on drugs. Where he lived, who he hung out with … he was strung out all the time…"

With a shake of his head, Jason reassured her. "I'm not judging her. Go on."

She swallowed hard. "I was sleeping one night and he broke in." Closing her eyes, her entire body shuddered under the weight of the obviously painful memory. "He tried to cajole me into splitting the money, and when that didn't work, he got angry. So angry."

Jason listened, knowing he wasn't going to like what came next. Knowing, too, he couldn't go back and prevent whatever it was she'd lived through.

She wrapped her arms around herself, rocking as she spoke. "He shook me and then his hands were around my neck, squeezing–" She forced her eyes open wide. "When he released me, I screamed. He said he'd be back for what was his and he took off."

A possessive fury took hold, that anyone would hurt this sweet woman whose smiles came so easily despite everything she'd been through.

"So what did you do?" he asked, his jaw clenched so his own anger didn't spill out and scare her. Because at this point he wanted to kill her brother.

"I ran. I packed up everything I could take with me overnight and disappeared. I figured New York City was the largest, easiest place to get lost. I started in a hotel, found a lawyer, changed my last name ... and here I am."

He blinked, knowing it couldn't have been that simple. "A name change is public record."

"Not when it's sealed because you can show the judge the fading bruises on your neck," she said, her hands coming up to clasp herself there.

Yep. He was going to fucking kill her sibling.

"So somehow he found you?" Jason asked, managing not to clench his fists and scare her away from *him*.

She nodded. "I'm guessing the slashed tire was a warning, though I have to admit, I'd hoped that was a freak neighborhood kid incident. But the vandalism and the brick? He wants me scared so by the time he comes in person, I'll give him whatever he wants." She'd lowered her hands from her neck, leaving red marks from where she'd made her point.

Jason had had enough. He stood up and walked over, pulling her into his arms because he needed the connection and felt certain she did, too.

She relaxed into him, her soft curves easing against his. He breathed in her sweet scent and held her as the trembling in her body eased. Too quickly, she pulled away.

"You aren't alone anymore. Got that?" he asked.

She glanced up at him. "I appreciate you helping me get things fixed here at the shop, but make no mistake. I'm very much alone."

He wasn't going to argue now. There would be plenty of time for that later, when she balked against what he was beginning to plan out for her in his mind.

He might not have wanted someone else to find their way into his emotional cocoon, but this woman had done it. There was no way he was leaving her to fend for herself now that he knew what she was up against. And if that meant fighting *her* in order to keep her safe, he'd do it in a heartbeat.

FAITH WATCHED AS Sam Fremont, a tall man with hair pulled back in a ponytail, and the workman he'd brought with him scrubbed the spray paint from her window. He'd called in a glass company, who'd sent a guy to measure her door. He'd then left to cut the glass and would return with the right size to fix her entrance. It was as if Jason Dare had spoken and all her problems were going away.

If only things were that easy.

She already understood he was more complicated than his surface grin led her to believe. A sister who'd conquered childhood leukemia, a college friend who'd died under mysterious circumstances, a nightclub and a life she knew nothing about. She wanted to know everything and that was dangerous.

Still, she owed him, and though she didn't think he truly felt that tit for tat was necessary, she did. If it was a date he wanted, then she'd go out with him. At this point, it could no longer hurt. Colton had already found her. He was probably watching her shop as all this activity occurred. Did it really matter if she went out with Jason after this? It was obvious the man was a part of her life, as her friend, at the very least.

He'd settled into a chair in the center of the shop, surveying the work going on around him. He'd already left once, returning with sandwiches and sodas for everyone. As the hours passed and he vacillated between returning messages on his phone and talking to the workmen he obviously knew, she grew more confused.

"Don't you have somewhere else to be?" she asked him.

He raised an eyebrow as if to say, *Really*? "Nowhere more important. I want to make sure the work here is done correctly and this place looks exactly the way you want it."

She appreciated his thoughtfulness, but he had to have better things to do than worry about her. "Okay, but I can handle that. I don't want to take up more of your day than I already have. I can stick around until the guys are finished, lock up, and head home."

He folded his strong arms over his chest, his olive-green Henley pulling tight over his muscles. "And do you think I'm going to leave you here alone after what you told me about your brother?"

She'd been pushing thoughts of Colton aside all day. "I have pepper spray on my keychain." The words sounded ridiculous, even to her.

She was no match for her brother, and if he was strung out? He'd have a wiry strength she couldn't handle. She knew that firsthand, memories of her hands trying to pull his wrists off her neck very clear in her mind.

"Okay, fine. I appreciate you making sure I get home safely." She'd be a fool to fight Jason's protective nature.

"You still don't get it. But you will." He shook his head, amusement warring with a more serious expression. "You're coming home with me, sweetness. I'm not leaving you here or in that shitty walk-up with a crappy lock your brother could break with one good kick."

"Hey! That's my apartment you're insulting!" And all she could afford.

"It's only an insult if I'm wrong." He studied her,

as if daring her to argue.

"I can't just move in with you!"

He sighed. "Fine. You need someone to vouch for me? We can call my partners. Or my sister. Or… Hey, Sam! Am I trustworthy?" Jason yelled out to the man who was just climbing down a ladder, her clean window staring back at her.

Sam strode up to them and looked from Jason to Faith and back again. "Best man I know. Take a look at this." Reaching into his pocket, Sam pulled out his phone, then began scrolling through his pictures.

"This is my girl." He turned the phone so Faith could see a picture of a grinning little pixie with a bright smile and a pom-pom hat on her bald head, no hair hanging down beneath the folded brim.

"She's beautiful," Faith said, sliding her finger over her face.

"And if it wasn't for this guy introducing us to his sister, I don't think my wife and I would have made it through the roughest parts of her illness." He shoved his phone back into his pocket.

Looking up at Jason from beneath her lashes, she caught a flush on his cheeks.

"It just so happens I could help you, man. But I'm glad Sienna could do her part. She loves fundraising and doing anything she can for kids who've been through what she has."

Faith would like to help her one day, when there was no danger following her around, she thought sadly. For now, though, she had to fight through her own problems and not bring them into other people's lives.

"Thanks, Sam." Jason all but dismissed his friend, who waved and walked back to the other guy helping him.

"So? Still think I'm a serial killer?" Jason asked her.

"I never said–"

"Oh, by the way, my cousin ate one of your marshmallow pops and went crazy for them. She'd like you to contact her about doing the party favors for her son's birthday party. So now I'm hooking you up with business. I really think you can trust me to keep you safe." He grinned at his smug proclamation.

She wanted to smack him ... and kiss him at the same time. He had her head spinning, and she knew that was his intention. To keep her off-balance and win her over at the same time. So she was too over-whelmed to say no to his proposition about her moving in with him.

But she had to be smart about things. "I'm not questioning your ability to keep me safe, I'm wonder-ing why you're taking me on as your responsibility?" Her tone along with her emotions sobered.

He grasped her hand and pulled her into the back

kitchen area, where they could be alone. Backing her against the prep counter, his big body hovered over hers.

"From the second we met, there was a connection between us. I felt it and so did you. Then I ignored your tire and my gut screaming it was more than vandalism, and this happened. Now I know I should have paid attention." He drew a deep breath.

So did she and his delicious cologne swept over her. She steeled herself against his appeal because what they were discussing now was deadly serious.

"There's a lot about me I don't talk about," he went on. "I'm not saying never, I'm just saying for now. All you need to understand is that I've been in this situation before, being able to possibly prevent something bad from happening and ignoring my gut. I won't do that again. So when I say you're coming home with me? I mean it."

This was the second time he'd mentioned the connection between them, and despite her wariness, she agreed that there was one. But if she went to his home, it had to be about necessity, not desire.

"Thank you." She appreciated his honesty and felt he deserved hers in return. "I'll come with you, but connection or not, we're not sleeping together."

An amused smirk pulled at that sexy mouth. "I was planning on giving you your own room."

"Oh." Now she felt stupid and her cheeks burned with embarrassment.

He brushed his hand down her cheek and her body trembled with awareness. "But if you get scared in the middle of the night, feel free to come sleep with me."

JASON GRITTED HIS teeth as they walked up the dark stairs to Faith's apartment so she could pack up her clothing and stay with him. The building was small and narrow, with plenty of dark corners for someone to hide in, and he was glad he was getting her out of here before something worse than building damage happened. Her brother would have to go through Jason in order to get to her.

While she disappeared into the bedroom to gather her things, he dialed Gabe, a man who had a private investigator on retainer. At this point, Jason was going to owe his cousin more than just money for the favors he was accruing, but it couldn't be helped.

"Gabe? I need a favor. Your private investigator? I have someone I need him to dig into. Colton Holland," he said, giving Gabe Faith's former last name. "Start in Cedar Pointe, Iowa, but I think he's here now. Drug addict, so he isn't hanging out with the best people in town. Whatever he can find on him, I need."

He went on to explain what had been happening with Faith so Gabe could give the PI the rundown. At best, Jason wanted her brother behind bars. At the very least, he intended to make sure he was out of Faith's life for good.

"I'm on it," Gabe said. "I'll have Jack Renault contact you personally so you can deal directly with him."

"Thanks, cousin."

"So much for not seeing her again," Gabe said, chuckling as he disconnected the call.

At that moment, Faith walked out of the bedroom, rolling a suitcase behind her. Jason shoved his phone into his back pocket. "Ready?" he asked her.

She nodded, letting him take the suitcase from her hand.

"Don't you have a club to run?" she asked.

"Yes. And two partners to help in case of emergencies. Getting you out of here and settled at my place is an emergency."

Her lower lip jutted out in a pout, and it was all he could do not to kiss her and taste that plump flesh for the first time. He understood she was frustrated with the situation, that doing as he said bumped up against her independent streak, but she was also smart and knew that he was right about her apartment and its location.

"Come on." He followed her out the door, waited

as she locked up, and together they headed for his car.

She settled into the plush seat, the sweet scent he'd come to associate with her filling the air around him. Little by little, in the smallest ways, she was making herself a part of his life. He broke into a sweat because despite how hard he was pushing her to move in and be safe, he was breaching his own defenses in the process.

She'd be living in his house, a room apart from him. And though he wanted her in his bed, he had a gut feeling once he tasted her, touched her, *had* her, she'd burrow so deep inside him, he'd never get her out. He'd never felt this way about any of the women he slept with before. There was something different about Faith and it shook him to his core. The core he was determined to protect from more pain and loss.

He cleared his throat. "So I have a doorman who won't let anyone up who isn't cleared on a list," he said into the silence that had overtaken them as he drove.

"That's good."

"I'll drive you to the store in the morning, and I can work from there during the day."

She froze, turning slowly in her seat. "You don't need to be by my side twenty-four hours a day."

One hand on the wheel, he glanced at her. "Do you want to be alone in the shop when your brother shows up?"

She sighed and shook her head. "No."

"Then me working from your store it is."

Before she could say another word, he turned into the parking garage beneath his apartment building. In silence, he guided her up the elevator, taking her silence as nerves.

They walked down the bright hallway, a stark contrast from where she lived. He unlocked the door and unset the alarm before letting her step inside.

"So here we are. I'll give you the code and a set of keys, but you're not going out alone. Not until your brother is behind bars. Speaking of, did you tell the police about him?"

He rolled her luggage inside, closed and locked the door.

"No. I didn't. If it wasn't Colton, I didn't want to send them after him and anger him even more. Besides, we have no proof it was him. If the police find fingerprints on the brick, they'll have evidence then. Can we stop talking about this?" She turned away and he stepped closer, placing a hand on her shoulder.

"Hey. It's going to be okay. Let me show you around the place," he said to distract her from her problems.

She perked up at the subject change. "Show me the palace," she said.

Grinning, he mock bowed and walked her through

the overly large apartment he'd rented. When the nightclub was starting up, he and the guys shared an apartment for the first six months until they realized they might kill each other. They'd spread out to their own places, and since the club started earning right away, with the addition of Jason's trust fund from his errant father, he'd moved into this gorgeous spread.

"The kitchen is fairly new and large for a Manhattan apartment," he said as they passed the entryway.

"Wow," she said, peeking inside. "This is amazing. Do you use it much?"

He shook his head. "Not my thing. I'm not home for meals very often. But while you're here, consider my kitchen your kitchen."

"You know I will. This is a great apartment. Big for Manhattan."

He nodded. "I rented this place because there were two extra-large bedrooms and my family is from Florida. This way my mom can come visit, and up until a few months ago, my sister would come by, too. Now she lives in New York City, as well."

"You mentioned your mother. What about your father?" Faith asked, as he walked through the living area with his large-screen television and ultra-comfortable oversized sofa.

"That is a long story for another time." One he wouldn't be getting into now. "But my mom insisted on flying up and helping me match colors so I could impress any women I brought home," he said with a grin. "Typical mom, she wants her kids married and settled." Savannah Dare might have gone the nontraditional mistress route herself, but for her children? She wanted the best.

"And will she get that?" Faith turned to him, looking up at him with those curious, gorgeous green eyes.

"Well, let's see. My sister went the untraditional route, getting pregnant first, but there's no question she and her husband, Ethan, are head-over-heels in love. Alex is married to a great woman and they had a baby girl recently." No point getting into the half-sibling thing now. He hoped she'd end the conversation there.

"And you're the eternal bachelor?" she asked, dispelling that optimistic thought.

"Something like that." Winking at her, he grasped her elbow and led her to the far side of the apartment, where the two bedrooms were located. "Come. You can check out your room."

He led her to the bedroom beside his, one his mother had decorated to *her* taste, with a – *cough* – bright floral comforter and matching valence above the window.

"Oooh, it's so pretty!" she said, grasping her suitcase from his hand and pulling it inside.

"I'll be sure to let my mother know you like it," he muttered. He'd never forgiven her for the flowered room, but he loved her anyway.

"Wouldn't that be admitting you brought a woman to your apartment?" she teased him before sitting down on the bed, her shoulders hunching over as she finally let herself relax.

"I was going to ask if you're hungry but you look beat."

She lifted her head. "I'm both. Would you mind if I shut my eyes for half an hour before we eat?"

"Of course not. I'll order us something. Do you want anything in particular?"

She shook her head as she kicked off her shoes. "You choose." She swung her feet up onto the bed, closed her eyes, and if he wasn't mistaken, she was out before she her head hit the pillow.

Jason headed to his bedroom, completely aware of the woman sleeping in the next room. He changed into a pair of sweats and a tee shirt, ordered a large pizza, and settled onto his couch, watching Sports Center on television.

He wasn't surprised to see a clip of his brother, Alex, on the screen. Once an NFL football player, he had been forced, on doctor's orders, to retire due to a severe concussion. He couldn't take the chance of another head injury without risking permanent damage. Seeing an opportunity, their half brother Ian, president of the Miami Thunder, ironically the opposing team to the one Alex had played for in Tampa, had offered him a job teaching players about preparing for the future beyond football. The program had been adopted by the NFL, and Alex did a lot of promotion and training around the country, including television interviews like the one Jason had just seen.

He lifted his glass of soda to his brother. "Go, you," he said to his sibling on TV.

A few minutes later, dinner arrived. He placed it on the table and walked back to where Faith slept. Cute little snores sounded in the room and he grinned.

Although she'd said to wake her, he didn't have the heart. She must have been so wiped out to fall asleep so fast, the stress of handling her brother alone for so long catching up with her.

He walked in, picked up an afghan blanket and covered her, standing like a creeper and watching her sleep. What was it about this woman that got to him?

Obviously she was beautiful, but Jason had been with his share of gorgeous women over the years, and he'd let them go when their time together came to an end. But Faith was more than pretty. Clearly she was strong. She'd picked up and left her home, coming to a big city and making her own way without help. She also hadn't lost her sense of humor during a difficult time, nor was she willing to give up her independence easily. All of which he admired. But there was so much more to Faith than any of that, and now he'd have the chance to see exactly what made her tick.

He'd wanted a date, and instead he had her under his roof, in the room next to his. He didn't like the reasons for their forced togetherness, but he sure as hell couldn't say he minded it. And that was a first for Jason Dare.

Chapter Four

FAITH MADE CANDY in the back of her shop alone since Kelsey had looked dead on her feet and Faith had sent her home early. She finished up and rushed to the counter, where she could be the face of Sweet Treats, selling her candy. She needed to hire another employee, but she had to make sure she could afford the expense. As long as things continued as they were, no more incidents like the vandalism, and she'd be okay.

She and Jason had had a frustrating discussion on the way to work about who would pay for the cleanup. So far she hadn't won, but she didn't want to be indebted to him any more than she already was. The man was giving her a place to stay in addition to fixing up her business. She wanted, no, needed to pay her own way.

Speaking of Jason, he had created an office for himself in a corner, out of the way but where he had a good view of the entrance and behind the counter. There was a back door leading to the alley off the kitchen, and he'd made sure she locked that tight, not letting her open it up for cool air to come inside. She knew better than to argue when he was right.

He'd set up his laptop, plugged it into the wall, had his iPad, his cell phone, and had been making and taking calls and FaceTiming with his partners all morning long, not seeming concerned in the least that he was doing business out of a candy shop and not his own nightclub.

Faith had called his cousin's wife, Isabelle, and she was coming over to talk about what she wanted for her son's birthday party. This would be branching out, another way to get her candy into new people's hands, and she was excited about the prospect.

This morning, with her new door and clear window, business was brisk, walking traffic bringing people inside, but by lunchtime, things slowed down, which worked for her because she could get off her feet.

Just as she was about to sit down across from Jason, a beautiful brunette walked into the store with a little boy in her arms.

"Uncle Jase!" the little boy yelled, wriggling in his mother's arms to get down.

She placed him on the floor and he ran to Jason, who swung the boy into his arms.

"Hey, champ!" How are you doing?" Jason asked,

lifting the boy into his arms and hefting him up on one hip.

"Good. Mommy said candy for my birfday."

Jason chuckled while Faith grinned at the adorable child.

"Sorry I'm late," the woman who must be Isabelle said. "I took him for lunch first, hoping to curb his appetite before we hit the candy store."

"It's fine. This is the first lull I've had all morning anyway. I'm Faith," she said.

"Call me Izzy."

"Tell you what," Jason said. "How about I take this kid for a tour and we'll handle any customers who come in while you two talk?"

"Are you sure?" Faith asked.

"It's fine. We're going to check out the candy."

"Candy!" the boy said with a fist pump.

"Not too much, Noah," Izzy said, eyeing Jason warily. "I have to deal with the sugar rush," she warned him.

Jason's grin was not to be trusted and Faith had a vision of him with his own kids one day. Oh, he'd insinuated he wasn't into bringing women home to his mother, but seeing him with this little boy, she had a hunch he'd want to change his mind one day. A wistful feeling curled inside her belly at the notion and she pushed it away. He was her friend doing her more favors than she had a right to expect. Thinking of him as a sexy man she desired would do nothing helpful in her current situation. Considering him as a potential father was an ovary-exploding way to get into trouble.

"Well, that expression tells me a lot," Izzy said, breaking into Faith's thoughts.

She blinked to return herself to the present. "I'm sorry. What did you say?"

Izzy grinned. "Basically that you have it bad for Jason. Not that I blame you. Those Dare genes are potent. I ought to know."

Faith's face flamed in embarrassment. "I don't... I didn't..."

"Oh, you so do." Izzy pulled out a chair and sat down at an empty table.

Faith joined her, still mortified she'd been caught daydreaming about and staring at Jason.

"But it looks to me like that attraction goes both ways. He's basically set up his office here. Gabe told me Jason's helping you out. No specifics, of course. But I can look at him, see how he keeps checking you out to make sure you're okay, and put two and two together."

"You don't beat around the bush, do you?" Faith asked, liking Jason's cousin by marriage already.

"I figure life's too short not to go after what you want. I took the long route to my destiny. I thought maybe I'd help you speed yours up," Izzy said with a grin.

Faith didn't want to burst her bubble, but the truth was a lot more boring than whatever Izzy was conjuring up in her mind. Although the chemistry was sizzling and the desire was mutual, he was taking care of her out of pity and a fear that something would happen to her that he'd have been able to prevent. She wanted to be more than an obligation to a man. That is, when her life calmed down enough to allow for her to let people in.

"Jason and I met by chance. He helped me with a slashed tire. It's been one situation after another since, and he's been nice enough to help me out. That's all that's going on between us."

"Keep telling yourself that. You'll be pleasantly surprised when things take a turn. Okay, so let's talk candy. That basket you gave Jason was delicious. The kids will go nuts for it and the moms will wish they'd thought of it. I'm having a party for Noah next weekend and I'd love it if you could make them up as party favors."

"I'd love to! If you want me to do something special for the kids, I could do that. If he has a theme for the party? I could work around that and do something more like the baskets for the adults."

"Paw Patrol. And I love both ideas."

Faith figured she'd be researching children's characters. She thought some more, then said, "I'd be happy to deliver them to the party and set them up on the table. Take some of the burden off of you. I'm sure you'll be busy enough that day." She could get Kelsey to run the store while she made the delivery and handled the decorative setup.

"You're so sweet! But Jason's coming to the party. Why don't you come with him and stay?"

"But I couldn't. It's family and friends…" She didn't belong there.

"Great idea, Iz," Jason called as he walked out from behind the counter. Noah had chocolate on his cheeks and a pop stick in his hand. "I was going to tell you I didn't want to leave Faith alone, and I wasn't sure if I could make it."

Faith rolled her eyes at his way of thinking. "It's over a week away." For all she knew, the police would link the break-in to Colton and pick him up before then. She didn't want to discuss the specifics in front of Izzy and her son and frighten them away. Colton was too big of a coward to come after her with people around.

"We'll both be there, Iz. Thank you. And here's your little sugar fiend. I kept it at two."

"I had free, Mommy!"

Izzy nodded and mock glared at Jason. "You listen

well," she said, her tone full of sarcasm. "Come to Mommy, baby. I'll clean your face." She pulled wipes from her purse and began cleaning the child's cheeks.

When she finished, she stood. "I've got to get this one home for a nap. Sometimes I still get lucky and he'll lie down ... although thanks to his uncle, I'm guessing today won't be one of those days." She turned to Faith. "It was a pleasure meeting you. I'm looking forward to seeing you at the party. Oh, maybe we can get lunch one day soon. Bye!"

Izzy left in a hurry and Faith shook her head, her smile wide as she thought about the other woman's fun personality. "I like her."

"Gabe likes her, too. Love at first sight, to hear them tell it, although it took years for them to get together. It was after Gabe's brother, Decklan, arrested her for grand theft auto. Long story," Jason said, chuckling. "I'm sure you'll hear it at the party."

She blinked in surprise. Not at his crazy family stories but about the party. "You were serious? You want me to come to a family event?"

He nodded, his hooded eyes taking her in.

She knew why he was dragging her along, and despite the practicality of the idea, it hurt her feelings at the same time. "So you can keep an eye on me and make sure I'm safe?"

She didn't know why that suddenly bothered her

so much when that was the basis for their relationship ... friendship. Whatever it was between them. But thinking on Izzy's words, how he looked at her, how she studied everything about him, from his easy stride to the way he took control with his partners, expressing what he wanted just forcefully enough to get them to agree with him without disagreeing first ... Jason Dare was a strong man she could come to rely on.

And as much as that scared her? It made her desire him, and she wanted him to feel the same way about her. Just temporarily. Because eventually, she would get back on her feet, Colton would be arrested, she hoped, and she'd go back to building her life here in New York. But while she was with Jason, was there anything wrong with acting on the simmering attraction?

She stepped closer to him, taking in the chocolate stain on his cream-colored shirt. "I can stay at your apartment and be perfectly safe there." If she was going to stay at that party beyond setup, he had to *want* her there.

"You're not staying home." A low growl made its way up his throat.

Her nipples puckered at the sexy sound. "Why not?

"Because." He moved in, his big body hovering over hers.

Body heat and his musky scent surrounded her, warmth and a tingling sensation dancing over her skin. "Because *why?*" He needed to say it. Needed to tell her he wanted her there.

Reaching out, he slid his hand behind her neck, his fingers gliding into her hair, tugging her head back as he said, "Because I want you there. I. Want. You."

JASON KNEW SHE was pushing him to admit what they both felt. What couldn't be denied. And he was through fighting the yearning for this woman. For as long as she needed his help and desired him, too, she was his.

He slid his tongue into her mouth and knew he was lost. Arousal ripped through him, hard and fast, the warmth of her mouth and the way she pressed her body into his turning him on. He tugged on her hair and she moaned, the vibrations rippling through him. She wound her arms around his neck and pressed her lush body against his, stripping away his defenses. With a groan, he tangled his tongue with hers, then pressed kisses and nibbles down the side of her neck, suckling on the sensitive spot behind her ear.

She gripped his hair, holding on as he devoured her, tasting her flesh and finding it as sweet as she was. His cock throbbed as desire consumed him, fast and furious, based on this one first kiss alone. He could go on like this forever, just feasting on her mouth, learning what she liked, imprinting himself on her.

But without warning, the tinkle of the doorbell interrupted them and she jumped, backing away from him, fixing her hair, and swiping her hand over her mouth, her cheeks flushed as she faced the customer in front of her.

"Umm… Hi. I just wanted to buy some candy," a woman said, stepping toward the door, her own face flushed.

"No, wait. I'm sorry. What can I get you?" Faith rushed behind the counter, leaving Jason with a hard-on the likes of which he'd never seen and the inability to speak. So he lowered himself into the chair in front of his laptop, drawing in a deep breath and hoping he could get back to work.

Long after the customer left the shop, Faith busied herself in the back, clearly avoiding him, which he let her do, knowing they'd be alone later tonight at his apartment. In the afternoon, the shop became busy, the after-school crowd tumbling in. Clearly word had gotten around and teenagers came and went, keeping Faith hopping.

At no time did Jason catch sight of anyone looking remotely suspicious, although he realized he needed a picture of her brother if he was going to recognize anyone stalking the premises. He checked in with the PI Gabe had given him and the man said he hadn't found any hint of Colton in the city. He'd tracked his movements in his hometown up to a week ago, after which he'd disappeared. But the man was still searching.

Finally, the end of the day came, and since Faith closed up at six during the week, only staying open later on the weekends, they could go home. He helped her clean up and close the store in silence. He understood she was still flustered by the kiss. Clearly she wasn't one of his more experienced women, and he both liked and appreciated that about her. She was unique, special, and got under his skin. And if her brother came near her, he'd have to answer to Jason.

They were settled in his car when he turned to her. They hadn't eaten since lunch and he was starving. "How about Italian for dinner?" he asked.

Her eyes lit up at the thought of food. "Sure."

"I know a great little place we can go. The owner is a friend of my cousin's. He introduced me to him when I moved to town and you'll love the food."

"Oh! You want to go out and not order in?" she asked, sounding surprised.

He chuckled. He wanted to talk to her in a setting where she couldn't escape to her room, make sure she understood that kiss had meant something.

"You owe me a date, sweetness."

Her face flushed and she turned to him. "Did I ever actually agree to go out with you?"

He reached over, because they were at a stoplight, and ran his knuckles down her cheek. "By moving in with me, it was implied that we'd have dinner together."

He drove them to a parking garage, left the car with the attendant, and strolled, his hand on the small of her back, to an old-fashioned northern Italian restaurant.

The owner, Gino, greeted him as they walked in the door. "Jason Dare, it's been too long! Rosa! Jason is here!"

A robust woman came out of the kitchen, rushing over to greet them. "Jason! Did you bring Gabriel?" she asked, giving him a kiss on the cheek.

"He's home with his family," Jason said. "But I did bring a friend. Faith, this is Rosa Bianci and her husband, Gino. She makes the best pasta in the city. This place is a hidden gem."

Rosa, an attractive older woman with dark hair, smiled at Faith. "Oh, what a pretty young lady. You finally brought a girl here to meet us!" She grasped Faith's cheeks and held her face in her hands. "So nice to have you here."

"It's wonderful to meet you," Faith said, finally

getting a word in. She shot Jason an amused glance, and he was pleased she wasn't put off by Rosa's friendliness.

He deliberately never brought women here. Rosa, who had taken an instant liking to him in part due to the fact that he was Gabe's cousin, and she loved Gabe and his family, would assume there was more going on than just a dinner. And Jason didn't want any woman he was with making that assumption as well. It spoke volumes that he didn't have a problem with Faith here now.

"Come," Gino said. "I have your special table and nobody's sitting there." He led them to a small corner in the back that Jason knew well.

"Sometimes I come here and sit in the corner and work," Jason explained. "This table is quiet."

"And you never bring women here. Interesting," Faith said under her breath.

Jason grinned as he held out her chair. She was going to grill him about his love life, he could see it coming. And he didn't mind answering. She already knew his mother hadn't met women in his life. Faith had a strong inkling as to what he was about. She just didn't know why he kept his emotions bottled up tight. If she asked, he would admit to some things, but not to all.

After ordering fried zucchini and a bottle of Pinot

81

Grigio wine, Jason leaned back in his seat and studied Faith. After a long day at work, she was still as pretty as he'd found her this morning when she walked out of her room, a smile on her face. He loved how she easily wore the Sweet Treats tee shirt, never worried about being dressed down, always comfortable in her own skin.

"So, how was your day?" he asked with an amused grin on his face.

She mock glared at him. "Are you looking to discuss that kiss?" she asked, surprising him that she broached the subject first.

Score one for her, he thought. Maybe he hadn't given her enough credit. "Only if you had issues with it."

"Issues like what? It was so good I want to do it again?"

Her admission both shocked and aroused him.

Her eyes opened wide at the words that had escaped. "And I haven't even had a glass of wine as an excuse for being so honest," she muttered with a shake of her head.

"Good thing I want to do it again, too," he said, deadly serious. He reached across the table and grasped her hand, his thumb running across her skin.

He let the silence surround them for a few moments before speaking again. "I admit I didn't plan for you, but you're here, you're in my life, and not only am I going to protect you, I'm going to have you," he said, his words as serious as the growing feelings that kept taking him off guard. "Any argument?" he asked.

She swallowed hard. "No."

"Good." Satisfaction rushed through him. He'd felt the power in that kiss and knew they were destined to do it again … and again. He wanted his mouth and tongue on other parts of her body, tasting the innate sweetness that was Faith.

"Wine!" Gino said, coming up to the table and uncorking the bottle. He poured some for Jason to taste.

He enjoyed the flavor and nodded. The older man filled each glass. The restaurant was starting to fill up, and he was glad they'd made it here in time to snag his favorite, more isolated table.

"Would it be okay if I brought out the house special?" Gino asked. "My Rosa would love to treat you and she cooked it with love."

Faith smiled at the older man. "That would be fine with me," she said.

"Me, too."

Gino strode off and Faith met his gaze. "So tell me, Jason Dare, what is your situation with women? You haven't wanted to introduce any to your mother, and these people are like close friends and they've never met one of your dates. I know you're not gay.

What are you hiding?" Faith tucked her hands beneath her chin, grinning as she put him on the spot.

He'd been prepared for this question, and he chose the easiest issue in his past to admit to. "My father's a bigamist. Or as close to being a bigamist as one can get without marrying both women at the same time."

He *hated* talking about Robert Dare. The man had raised Jason and his siblings, had been there for them, and he'd thought they had a great family ... only to discover the truth.

"I'm sorry ... what?" Faith asked, stunned as any rational person would be.

"My father had another family with a woman he was legally married to, and five kids, including me, while he had an affair with my mother and raised me and my siblings with her. She knew, or found out, and stayed with him anyway." A pain throbbed in his temple as it always did when this subject came up. But it was nothing compared to the pain of losing his best friend, so as much as it hurt, he would stick with this part of his past for now.

"Wow. That's ... awful. I'm sorry," Faith murmured.

He nodded. "It's complicated. He married Emma St. Claire as part of a merger of two families. It wasn't a love match, and instead of trying to create one, my father, Robert, met my mom and fell in love. I think that's how he justified what he did." Jason shook his head. "Although we didn't know it at the time, he told his other family that he was traveling on business for his hotels when he was really with us." He swallowed hard. "He missed major events in their lives like graduations and birthdays but came to ours. Again, justifying it because he was in love with my mother and not theirs."

"What a pig," Faith muttered honestly and Jason managed a laugh.

"Truer words were never spoken," he said.

"How did you find out?"

He took a long sip of wine and she did the same. "Well, that's where Sienna's illness comes in. She had been diagnosed with leukemia. Chemo and treatments didn't work, so they wanted to do a bone marrow transplant. None of us were matches, so Robert decided to go to his *other* family and ask them to be tested."

Faith had leaned in, utterly engrossed in the story, and he didn't blame her.

"He dropped the bomb on his legitimate family, destroyed them, and yet his wife ... Emma ... was gracious enough to test her kids. Avery, the youngest, was a match, and she donated her bone marrow to my sister."

Jason recalled those difficult days and sighed. "I

guess you could say I was left with a bad taste in my mouth for relationships and issues with trust." He also had a problem fearing that the people he loved would leave him, which stemmed from his father's behavior as well.

"All the siblings have made their peace with each other. The girls are the closest but we're all a family."

"And your parents? What's their story now?" Faith asked.

Jason scowled. "My father is currently in love with another woman and in the process of divorcing my mother. It's been difficult," he said, swirling the wine around in the glass. "My mother knew about his first wife. She got my father by cheating, not that she knew it when the relationship began. But now she's losing him the same way."

Faith glanced at him. "You really haven't had the best example of a stable marriage or family, have you?" she murmured.

He shook his head. Although if he had to dig deep, he'd say that Levi's death had impacted him far more as an adult than his father's betrayal. "There's so much more," he admitted. "But I'm not really up to talking about it now," he said, bracing himself for her to push harder for more information.

"I respect that," she said gently. "Everything in its time."

He blinked, shocked that she didn't ask for more answers when he knew how curious she must be. Yet she respected his barriers, and for that he was grateful.

"Dinner!" Gino said, showing up just in time as far as Jason was concerned.

The enjoyed a delicious gnocchi along with their fried zucchini and homemade cannoli for dessert. By the time they'd finished eating, Faith finally looked like she was drooping where she sat, exhaustion beginning to catch up with her.

"Are you ready to go home and get some sleep?" he asked.

She nodded. "But I was wondering if we could stop by my apartment? I forgot to pick up some extra work shirts, and I'm too tired to wash and dry this one tonight."

"Of course." He'd get her in and out of there quickly, so she could go back to his place and get some sleep.

But when they arrived at her building and walked up the darkened stairway, they discovered her door had been taped up because someone had clearly kicked it open. The wood had splintered and there was yellow tape across the door.

"Oh my God!" Faith reached for one of the strips, obviously determined to get inside, but Jason grabbed her around the waist and pulled her back.

"Hang on. We have no idea what happened. Do you have a landlord?"

Before she could answer, a bald man with a large beer belly came striding toward them from the other side of the hall. "It's about time you came back," he said, scowling and clearly pissed off.

"Mr. Donovan, what happened?" Faith asked.

"The neighbors said they heard a noise in the middle of the night, and the next day your door was shattered."

"Nobody came out to check on the unusual sound?" Jason asked in disbelief. His gut instincts about this neighborhood had been spot on.

The heavyset man shook his head. "You're going to pay to fix the door, young lady."

Jason stepped into the man's personal space. "That's Ms. Lancaster to you. And how about you back off. Did you call the cops?"

"Not my job, not my problem."

"It'll be your problem if any of her things are missing and no one reported it. She's not fixing your door, either. That's your goddamn job." Jason pushed past the other man and gingerly removed the tape put up over her door.

"Jason, it's fine. I'll deal with it later," Faith said.

Donovan shook his head and, grumbling, walked back the way he came.

Jason held her hand and led the way into an apartment whose contents had been turned upside down and ripped to shreds.

Chapter Five

FAITH HELD ON to her composure by a thread, but she was determined not to let Colton get to her. She'd survive this like she had everything else he'd done to her. Through sheer grit and determination.

She stepped over the sofa pillows he'd tossed onto the floor, the books he'd flipped through and ripped, and the contents of drawers left open that he'd rifled through. She wasn't sure why he thought she'd be stupid enough to leave money around the house, but that was a desperate addict's thought process.

"Are you okay?" Jason asked, his hand in hers, his body a solid presence by her side.

"Yes." She straightened her shoulders. "There was nothing here for him to find."

"At a glance, is anything missing?"

For the first time, she looked beyond the mess on the floor. She had a small television she'd taken from her room at home in Iowa that sat on the counter in the kitchen. Gone.

She swallowed hard. "Television is gone. My laptop would probably have been gone if I didn't bring it with me to work." And her laptop contained all of her business files, so she was grateful for that.

"Any jewelry?" he asked.

"I keep a small box beside my bed. It has a few necklaces, and… Oh my God. Mom's necklace!" She broke free from his grasp and ran for the small bedroom, which hadn't fared any better than the living area.

Her bed had been ripped apart, her clothes tossed, probably just for spite, and as she knelt down beside the small night table she'd bought at a secondhand store, her heart stopped. The doors were swinging open, and inside, where her beloved jewelry box had been, was empty.

"It's gone." That's when all the strength she'd been holding on to fled. "The one thing I had left of my mother is gone."

Jason knelt down beside her. "We'll find it," he promised.

She glanced up at him, feeling the tears shimmer in her eyes, but she couldn't control them. The pain of losing her mother was always there, just below the surface, yet she had no choice but to keep moving forward.

This was a blow that hurt. "You can't know that." She looked into his serious eyes.

"I know I can do my best. We need to outthink him. I bet he pawns it for cash. If you have a photograph of it? Or if not, if you can describe it, my private investigator will look for it in nearby pawnshops."

"Private investigator?" Her legs cramped and she rose to her feet. He followed and they sat down on her messy bed.

"Jack Renault. I have him looking for your brother. I wanted to know if he was in the city, although I think there's no doubt. He's just good at going underground." Jason frowned, his frustration at her situation obvious.

"You barely know me and you hired a PI? You're letting me stay in your apartment. I don't understand."

"I'm not sure I do, either, but here we are." He lifted a hand, his knuckles stroking her cheek. "You're safe with me."

Her stomach pitched with unexpected desire for this man. She said the only thing she could. "Thank you."

He treated her to a sexy smile but quickly sobered. "We should call the police."

She nodded, knowing it was going to be a long night.

✧   ✧   ✧

A WEEK HAD passed since the break-in. The police

had no solid leads and neither did Jason's investigator, so Jason kept Faith close and they went about their lives. He'd taken time off from the club in the evenings, but he had a plan to implement and his friends were getting antsy, wanting him to come by and see the work that had been accomplished so far. He hadn't wanted to leave Faith home alone, and given how exhausted she was after work, he'd sacrificed his own business needs.

This weekend was Noah's birthday party, and she'd been working hard all day on the treats and packaging she had planned for the event. The good news was that she had Kelsey back at work and she wasn't handling the burden of everything on her own.

The bad news was they were both tiptoeing around the sexual frustration that was building between them. Living together made for very close quarters. More than once, he'd walked out of his bedroom in his boxers, stumbling to the kitchen for a drink, forgetting he had company, and found her in the living room on her computer because she'd been unable to sleep.

She, too, had thought she'd be alone and was dressed in a pair of short shorts and a flimsy camisole top, her abundant breasts falling out of the lace edging. He'd woken up at the sight, his dick getting hard in an instant. She'd been flustered and apologized, rushing back to her room, but not before he caught the way her gaze fell to the bulge in his underwear and a beautiful, sexy flush stained her cheeks.

Jason had never hesitated to take what was offered, but that was the issue here. He wasn't sure how much Faith was offering. She was under a ridiculous amount of stress, and he didn't want to take advantage of her vulnerable situation. On the other hand, he recognized the signals that told him she was interested in him and he damned well wanted her. He'd gone so far as to take a cold shower before heading back to bed after their run-ins because he desired her that much. The question was, how much more could either of them take before they broke and ended up in bed?

He watched her from a chair that must have his ass imprint on it by now, as she put away the candy on the shelves, humming as she worked, breasts bouncing in the confines of her tee shirt, and he groaned.

Finally, after she'd locked up for the day, they were in his car on the way home. He'd been about to ask her what she wanted for dinner when his phone rang. He hit send and said hello.

Landon's voice sounded over the intercom in the vehicle. "When are we going to see your ugly face?" his friend asked.

Jason chuckled, glancing at Faith's amused expression. "Sorry, man. I've been tied up. I explained it to you already."

"Well, get untied and get your ass down to the club. We're overdue for a group meeting. You're the one who wanted to expand, and we're the ones making it happen."

Jason winced because they were right. "I'll be there tonight," he promised, disconnecting the call.

Faith turned toward him, and though he kept his eyes on the road, he felt her narrowed stare.

"Your partners are annoyed. Do they know why you haven't been to work? And why didn't I even think about the fact that you had somewhere to be at night?" She groaned. "You were so busy during the day I forgot you ran a nightclub in the evening." She twisted her hands together, working herself up with a heap of self-blame and recrimination.

He placed a calming touch on her thigh, immediately aware of the soft heat of her body, and the desire he'd been fighting off and keeping at bay made itself known.

"I make my own choices," he said in a gruff voice. "And I wanted to be with you. Now I can drop you off at the apartment before heading to the club. I know with Christopher, my night doorman, on duty you'll be safe. I've just always felt better being there myself. Especially after your apartment was broken into."

She shook her head. "I'll come with you. It's the

least I can do. You don't need to make another stop just for me. Besides, it'll be fun to see you in your element."

She grinned at him and he laughed. "Fine, but don't take anything the guys say to heart. Tanner, especially, can be an ass." Because he'd never gotten over Landon's loss. None of them had but they each dealt in their own way.

"I can deal with it."

He knew she could. She'd been holding up like a champ so far. She'd even dealt well with the robbery, although the loss of the necklace put a dent in her armor. Jason had called Jack Renault, and the PI was looking for the jewelry based on Faith's description and an old photograph where the piece was shown from a distance on her mother's neck. Lord knew there were a lot of pawnshops in New York City for him to scour, and the process would take time.

They walked into the club well past suppertime, when people came for after-dinner drinks and the Friday night crowd had started picking up. He gestured for Faith to head upstairs ahead of him, following close behind, and they entered the main office area to find Tanner and Landon dressed for a night on the floor.

"Well, well, well. Look who's here," Tanner said.

"Thanks for coming. We know you have other

things on your mind right now," Landon said, his gaze falling to Faith.

"I suppose introductions are in order. Faith Lancaster, these are my best friends and partners, Landon Bennett and Tanner Grayson." Jason gestured between them.

"Nice to meet you," she said.

"At least now I understand Jason's reasons for being tied up elsewhere," Tanner said, laughing.

Jason shot his friend an annoyed glare.

"It's nice to meet you, too, Faith." Landon had always had better manners than Tanner, who was only a charmer when he wanted to be one.

"Jase, we need to talk," Tanner said bluntly, his stare on Faith.

Jason rolled his eyes at the man's rude behavior.

"I can go downstairs," she offered, eyeing the crowded bar area with little to no enthusiasm.

"Sweetness, how about I set you up in my office for a few minutes?" Jason asked, offering her a more palatable option. She didn't need to be surrounded by strangers at the moment, and his asshole friend should know better.

"Sure. That'd be great." Her shoulders relaxed and she was clearly relieved.

He placed a hand on her back and led her to his private office. "Make yourself comfortable. I won't be long. These guys … they just need a group hug sometimes." Chuckling, he winked at her. "And Tanner's bark is worse than his bite. Honestly." He leaned in and brushed a kiss on her cheek, her sweet scent and warmth calling to him. "I'll be back.

He strode back into the room and glared at Tanner. "Do you have to be an asshole?"

"Sorry," he muttered. "I just thought it'd been awhile since the three of us had gotten together. I didn't expect you to show up with her."

"She's in danger. Her drug addict brother broke into her apartment last week. I told you this. Come on." He placed a hand on Tanner's back. The man held on to the three of them like a lifeline, and Jason should have realized he needed to come down here long before now.

Tanner narrowed his gaze. "Who is she to you, Jase?"

He ran a hand through his hair and met his friend's gaze. "I wish to God I knew. I don't believe in love at first sight, but I haven't slept with her and she already means something to me. And trust me, I tried like hell to keep an emotional distance. You know me. You know I keep people out and why. We all do."

Landon strode over and placed a hand on his shoulder. "If she's important to you, then we all step up to help. Right, Tanner?"

The other man grumbled but nodded. He was always the last to come around when it came to outsiders in their small circle. Which was weird, since Landon had lost his twin, but Tanner's life hadn't been an easy one in all ways.

"I appreciate it. Now as for the club, how are the improvements coming?" Jason walked over to the glass window that overlooked the downstairs bar area, which had grown even more crowded since he'd arrived.

Bartenders were serving drinks, people mingling and dancing, as if they didn't have a care in the world. All in all, a perfect Friday night at Club TEN29.

"We're coming along at a faster pace than expected. Audio guys had an opening in their schedule, so they've upgraded the speakers and sound system. They've been able to work during the day since we open at night. No issues." Landon strode over to the bar. "Soda water?" he asked, glancing from Jason to Tanner.

"Not for me."

"Me, neither." Tanner shook his head. "Security's also been upgraded. You need to switch the app on your phone and you'll be able to see the new cameras and the areas we can watch."

"So now it comes down to acts, scheduling, and launch dates," Landon said.

Jason frowned. He wasn't ready to make decisions on who he wanted to open the new direction of their club, especially when it came to using Charlotte, his ex. "Let me talk to Grey," he said. Avery's husband was a safer bet and as big a draw.

"I have a list but it'd mean reaching out to managers, so see what you can get from your brother-in-law."

"Are you staying for the night?" Tanner asked.

"I'd like to see how Faith is feeling before I decide ... if you don't mind." He glanced at his partners.

"So that's how it is already?" Tanner snickered and Landon shot him a dirty look.

"It's fine. We can handle a regular night here."

His friends were solid, Jason thought. Even Tanner, despite his tendency to dig at a person's weakness.

"I'll hang for another few minutes. If you think of anything else you want to discuss, let me know." Faith was safe in his office.

But he needed to find her brother and get back to his life before he was so wrapped up in hers he lost track of what was important to him.

✦   ✦   ✦

FAITH SAT AT Jason's desk, waiting for him to return. She'd looked through her phone, checked her apps, which were minimal because she'd deleted all her personal social media accounts when she left Iowa, and now she had nothing else to do but look around at the man's office space. The room was similar to the larger area where the other two men had been waiting for them. Sleek chrome borders accentuated glass desks along with black and chrome chairs. Modern area rugs lay over natural wood floors that had a deliberately stripped, gritty look.

Although she never intended to pry, her gaze fell to the pictures along the far edge of the desk. There was an obvious family shot of Jason in the middle of a group of men and women, many of whom had similar features and who had to be his siblings. There was a wedding photograph of an older couple she presumed were his parents and a picture of a much younger Jason, Tanner, and Landon and another man identical to Landon in front of a statue. His twin she'd seen on the website, to whose memory the club had been dedicated.

She felt for all three of the men. With her mother's passing, she understood loss, and theirs had happened way too young. It didn't escape her notice that Jason never discussed that part of his past with her. Never mentioned Levi or the fact that they'd named the club after him. She wished he'd unburden himself. He'd already done so much for her, and she just knew if he talked about the pain he kept so close to his heart and carefully walled off, it might help.

As she frowned, her gaze traveled to the last picture. A photograph of an attractive woman with blonde hair with a little boy in her arms. Faith had no idea who the female was, and an unexpected knot of jealousy formed in her stomach. It was silly. She trusted that Jason wasn't married. He obviously lived alone, and he'd made his views on relationships crystal clear. There was no doubt he possessed an inherent protective streak from which she was currently benefitting despite him keeping most people at a distance. And yet there was this woman and child he'd never mentioned.

She rubbed her hands against her denim-clad thighs, growing antsy sitting here with nothing to do while Jason met with his partners, but she owed him at least this and much more. So she leaned back in the chair and relaxed herself, accepting she might be here awhile.

She began to doze off when the sound of the door opening startled her awake. She jumped in her seat, her heart doing a rapid pounding of fear inside her chest.

"It's okay, it's just me," Jason said, stepping into the room and closing the door behind him.

Her mouth tasted dry, like cotton. Although was used to it, waking often in the middle of the night in such a state, she was surprised she'd fallen asleep and dreamed here.

"I guess I had a nightmare about Colton and then the creaking of the door and the noise downstairs scared me. You just took me by surprise," she said, catching her breath, as she rose from her seat.

"I think that answers my question," he said cryptically from the doorway.

He was a welcome sight, handsome and sexy, in his dark jeans and black shirt.

"What question?" she asked, confused.

"I was going to ask if you wanted to eat something here and hang out downstairs at the club for a while, but I don't think the crowd and the noise is a good idea. We'll order something in back at my apartment." He strode up to her, joining her behind the desk.

"But your partners–" She shook her head. She didn't want the men to resent her more than they already did. Or at least, more than Tanner seemed to.

"Shh." Jason touched a finger to her mouth, then removed it, leaned in, and replaced it with his mouth, gliding his lips over hers.

She blinked in surprise, then leaned into the kiss, softening against him. He licked the seam of her lips and she parted, letting him in. At the touch of his tongue to hers, she forgot everything but the warmth and feel of him, the butterflies in her stomach, and the excitement suddenly racing through her veins. Desire replaced her earlier fear and she lost herself in his thorough, devouring kiss.

He raised a hand to her hair, tangling his palm in her ponytail, using the pull to tug her head to the side so he could deepen their connection. She couldn't remember the last time she'd had a long, leisurely, *arousing* kiss that seemingly had no end. She let everything go but the pure enjoyment of being so close to this man she'd wanted for so long.

The long nights of sleeping in a room near his, wondering if he slid naked beneath the sheets, of running into him in the family room in his boxer briefs, his state of arousal upon looking at her clear, finally caught up with her. She braced her hands on his cheeks and kissed him for all she was worth, dropping her walls and her guard for this one moment in time. When he finally released her kiss-swollen lips, she was dazed.

"Good," he said in a desire-laden voice. "You're relaxed now."

She narrowed her gaze. "Is that why you kissed me? Because I was worked up and frightened?"

His eyes darkened. "I kissed you because I've been wanting to do that for days. But the end result? Yeah, that's what I was aiming for. Ready to go home?" He slid his fingers into hers and she curled her fingers around his bigger hand.

"Ready."

"Then let's go."

She glanced away from his potent stare, her gaze coming to rest on the bulge in his pants. The erection he couldn't hide.

She slid her tongue over her lips, well aware of the pulsing deep inside her core.

"Don't look at me like that or I'll take you right here in my office. With my partners next door," he said in a gruff voice that wreaked havoc on her senses.

And she knew she was so aroused, she just might let him. So she grabbed her purse and rushed out the door.

✧   ✧   ✧

AFTER ARRIVING BACK at the apartment, they ordered in Italian food, ate, discussed his issues at the club, and never mentioned the kiss. It didn't matter that Jason's lips on hers was at the forefront of Faith's mind, or that she wanted to take things further; he was back to being the perfect gentleman. It was as if he'd used the kiss to jerk her back to reality and ground her in sensations other than fear, but he wasn't going to act on the arousal he'd inspired now.

Unsure of what to do, she was taken off guard when he said he'd clean up and instructed her to turn in and get a good night's sleep. Since he seemed to need the time alone, she nodded and strode out, struggling with her conflicting desires. The need to keep a distance from Jason so it was easy to walk away when this was over and the yearning she felt for Jason Dare.

She washed up and undressed, changing into a pair of her soft shorts and camisole. She crawled into bed, hating to admit that Jason had been right and she was exhausted...

Faith awoke to hands around her neck, her brother's face in front of hers, his breath fetid. "You know what I want, Faith."

She coughed but the sound strangled in her throat. How did he expect her to answer him if he was choking her to death? "Colton."

"The money. It's half mine and I want it."

She shook her head. Mom left it to me, *she thought, knowing better than to waste her breath. Precious air she wasn't getting. "Can't breathe." Spots danced in front of her eyes, fear spiraling inside her.*

He loosened his grip enough for her to draw in a painful breath. "Get me my money. I'll be back, and next time I expect you to give me what's mine."

Faith woke up choking, unable to breathe until she realized it had just been a dream. A real dream, but a nightmare that wasn't happening now. She was safe. She blew out a breath and lifted her hair off her neck. It wasn't the first time she had this nightmare and it wouldn't be the last. Most nights she went into the living area and worked on her business plans, knowing sleep would be impossible after the nightmare, but tonight there was another option on her mind.

She needed comfort and she wanted a pair of strong arms around her to reassure her everything would be okay. Jason's arms. More than solace, though, she desired him more than any man she'd ever met. And he'd admitted to wanting her.

She understood he had demons and past hurt and pain he hadn't yet come to terms with. He didn't want a relationship, didn't want the happily ever after she dreamed of having one day when she was free of Colton. She didn't want to be alone forever, even if she didn't allow herself to think of having friends and people in her life again now.

So she knew the score. She wouldn't be going into whatever this was with Jason with stars in her eyes, thinking she could change him. They were two consenting adults who desired each other. When her brother was behind bars, they'd go their separate ways. End of story.

But they had *now*.

Drawing a deep breath for courage, she made her

decision and walked out of her room and turned to go into his. She opened the door, glad when it didn't squeak, shut it behind her, and tiptoed quietly up to the bed. Then she had a silent debate with herself once more. Clothes on? Or clothes off?

There was nothing stopping her except her lack of courage, so she drew another long breath and slipped off her shorts and panties, then pulled her shirt over her head. There. She was naked, and before she could change her mind, she climbed onto the bed and slid up behind him, finding him as nude as she was. Drawing a deep breath, she wrapped her arms around his waist.

He shifted but didn't wake up. So she cuddled closer, finding comfort in his warmth. She really didn't want to disturb his sleep, something she desperately needed herself. He'd wake up, find her here, and realize what else she wanted come morning. She'd deal with her mortification at what she'd done then.

She lay her cheek against his broad back, inhaled his masculine scent, and began to breathe slowly, matching his tempo and finally relaxing enough to fall asleep.

Chapter Six

J ASON WOKE UP surrounded by heat. Not normal heat, where his comforter was too hot or the temperature was too high, but warm heat covering him. Suspecting but not wanting to assume, he opened his eyes.

He lay on his back, his arm around Faith, her head in the crook of his arm, her knee across his body ... and her pussy pressing against his thigh.

She was naked.

And since he normally woke up with a hard-on, it was no surprise that this morning's was extra ... hard. To say he was shocked she was here was an understatement. To find her naked was a sweet surprise he didn't want to question.

And yet he had to.

He kissed her lips once, twice, and waited for her to wake up.

Finally, sleepy green eyes opened and met his gaze. "Hi," she said, her cheeks turning an adorable pink.

"Hi?" He deliberately phrased it as a question.

"I guess you're wondering what I'm doing here?"

He chuckled. "That would be one of my questions."

"I had a nightmare and I didn't want to be alone." She drew a deep breath. "And since you told me you wanted me once and since you kissed me last night, I decided to tell you what I wanted."

"By getting naked." He didn't want to focus on the fact that she had nightmares. The idea of her hurting and afraid gutted him.

"By getting naked." A sudden playful, wicked gleam flickered in her eyes. "Can you think of a better way to express myself?"

He now had confirmation of both her desire and her consent. He wouldn't be taking advantage of a woman in a vulnerable situation, one who was relying on him, who was unsure of what she wanted. That's why he'd sent her to bed last night. So he didn't act on the raging desire to pick up where they'd left off with that kiss after she'd been afraid. She'd now had an entire night to reconsider. She was all in.

Which meant the mental restraints that had been holding him back were gone. He slid his arm out from beneath her, raised himself up, and covered her body with his own. His cock was cushioned between her thighs, his entire body on high alert.

Hands braced on either side of her head, he

pushed himself up and looked into her eyes. They'd grown hazy with need. One that was matched by the pulsing desire thrumming through his veins.

"I take it you're not mad?" A hint of vulnerability sounded in her voice.

He couldn't tear his gaze from her full lips. Lips he wanted to devour again. Answering her question was easy. "A naked woman I want crawls into my bed. No, I'm not mad." He let out a low laugh that came out sounding more like a growl of need. "Besides, does it *feel* like I'm mad?" He swiveled his hips and ground his cock into her sex.

She whimpered with need, and he dipped his head and pressed his lips against hers. Tasting her filled something inside him, an emptiness he hadn't been aware existed. Just like finding her on the side of the road felt *important*, so, too, did this moment.

She opened her mouth and let him in. Warmth and need surrounded him, along with a dizzying sensation that this was right. He kissed her long and hard before lifting his head and pushing his body down lower, needing to taste her everywhere.

"Do you taste sweet, candy girl?" he asked, swiping a tongue over her nipple.

She shuddered and he went to work, teasing the bud that tightened with every lick, suck, and graze of his teeth. She threaded her fingers into his hair and pushed his head down, silently asking for more. He bit down lightly on that pebbled nipple, then licked his way across her chest and over her other breast until he found the other one, giving it the same at times tender, at other times torturous treatment.

She moaned, pulling at his hair. "Jase, that feels so good."

So she liked nipple play, did she? Could she come from that alone? Not many women could. He hadn't been with any, but she was rubbing herself against him and urging him on. Willing to do anything to please her, he suckled on her nipple, cupping the other full breast in his hand and tweaking it with his thumb and forefinger. First hard, then soft, his hand played with her while his mouth worked on the other breast.

He took his time, enjoying how she moaned and writhed beneath him. His cock was so fucking hard, teasing her sex and torturing him at the same time, but that wasn't his focus. Not yet.

He lifted his head and began to rub her nipples gently, looking into her eyes. "Come for me, sweetness. I want to see you find pleasure."

He picked up her hand and pulled her fingers into his mouth, sucking on the digits until they were wet. "Play with yourself," he told her. "Show me what feels good." He dipped her other hand's fingers into his mouth and dampened them as well.

Her cheeks flushed, but as he rolled his hips into hers, she moaned and got to work. She plucked and pulled at her nipples, her entire body trembling as she gave herself pleasure. He got off watching her, his dick throbbing as she continued her assault on the tender buds.

"Oh, God." The words came out on a slurred moan. "So good."

"Keep going." His hips jerked against her sex, over and over, and if he couldn't hold on, he was going to come like a fucking teenager who couldn't control himself.

He didn't know if it was his grinding against her clit that he was unable to control or the pinching and pulling of her nipples, but she uttered a slow moan and her body trembled beneath him.

"I'm coming. Oh, God, yes." She released her hold on her nipples and grasped his shoulders, her hips lifting and thrusting against his.

He'd never seen a sexier, more beautiful sight than her coming apart, cheeks flushed, eyes fluttering closed. He waited until the shuddering stopped and she collapsed before rising and stripping off his boxers.

He came back over her, his cock hovering by her neatly trimmed sex. Then the obvious hit him. "Shit, condom." He always used protection. It was stupid and irresponsible not to.

"I'm on the pill." She bit down on her lower lip. "And I was at the doctor shortly before I left town." She looked up at him with wide green eyes, asking with her gaze if he was safe.

Because she trusted his answer and that meant the choice was his. He'd never wanted to feel a woman bare around him before Faith, and the knowledge rocked him to his core.

"I'm clean." He'd been tested for his yearly physical a few months ago and hadn't been with anyone since.

In response, she spread her legs beneath him and her trust was humbling. Her gaze never left him as he grabbed his cock, pumping the length with his fist before positioning himself at her entrance and gliding into her with a smooth thrust.

He felt her everywhere, his entire body aware of her slick inner walls, the heat of her surrounding him, and the vulnerable way her eyes opened wide as he filled her. A heavy lump formed in his throat, and he brutally pushed it aside, doing everything he could to focus on the physical sensations and not the emotional fallout of having sex with Faith. He refused to call it making love. That thought would send him running.

He was already invested. He couldn't let himself go *there*.

"Jason, move."

Faith's voice took him out of his self-reflection, and he did as she said, began to pump his hips back and forth, gliding in and out, riding the high he felt from being with her. Shifting positions, he deliberately thrust hard, hitting a different spot inside her, and she moaned aloud.

"Yes, there."

With that, he began a steady rhythm, taking them both for a hard ride. She grasped his cheeks and pulled him toward her. His lips came down hard on hers and he continued to pump into her. It wasn't long before his balls drew up tight, his spine tingled, and just as he knew he was going to come, she cried out his name.

He let himself go, spilling into her and losing a part of himself at the same time.

✧　✧　✧

FAITH RUSHED TO get ready for Noah's birthday party, knowing she and Jason had to stop at the shop and pick up the goodie boxes she'd put together yesterday. Because her clothes were in the closet in the guest room, she had a break from Jason's intense stare. He'd been watching her ever since this morning, as if trying to figure out just what had occurred between them in bed.

She'd like to know that herself. Intense didn't

begin to cover it. Life altering might come closer. Reminding herself this was a temporary relationship no matter how close to him she might feel, she finished putting on her makeup, fluffed her hair, drew a deep breath, and stepped into her bedroom. She dressed in a pair of black slacks and a white top, not wanting to call attention to herself at the party. She felt as if she were there to help set up her candy, and though she might also be there with Jason, she wasn't foolish enough to think she was truly an invited guest. Izzy was just being nice when she'd asked her to come.

It would be more than foolish to act like she was Jason's date at his nephew's birthday party and let the heady mix of being on his arm after being in his bed feed dreams that would never happen.

She took a quick glance in the mirror, well aware her cheeks were flushed ... because her body was still quivering with awareness from the orgasms ... plural ... he'd given her this morning. She picked up her purse and walked out of her room in his apartment, meeting up with him in the family room.

Her gaze slid over him, and though she did her best not to ogle, it was difficult. He looked sexy in a pair of dark jeans and a navy turtleneck shirt, those indigo eyes looking through her, his expression knowing. As if he could see her heart and know how fast it was beating just for him.

"Are you ready?" he asked.

She nodded, glancing at the time on her phone. "If we leave now, we have enough time to get the goodies and for me to set them up." She started for the door ahead of him, startled when he grasped her arm and spun her back to face him.

"What?" The word barely left her mouth when he wrapped one arm around her back, pulled her against him, and sealed his lips over hers.

All her worries and anxieties fled in the wake of his kiss. He devoured her with his mouth, licking, tasting, owning, and possessing, before letting her up for air.

"Better than breakfast," he said, setting her on her feet but holding on until she'd caught her breath.

She blinked, still somewhat dazed.

"Just needed a taste," he explained, gesturing toward the door. "Ready?"

She managed a nod. He picked up a birthday present off the counter, and off they went.

Much later, after she'd loaded her van, to Jason's complaining about how it was an old piece of shit and he wished she drove something safer, they arrived at his cousin Gabe and Izzy's apartment. It took them three trips to carefully carry everything upstairs. Kelsey was running the shop, so Jason helped, this time listening to her grumbling about how it was her job and she could do it herself.

They'd arrived with the last of her goodies when Izzy greeted them at the door, kissing Jason on the cheek and pulling Faith inside. "Come. Let's set up so we can have fun."

Izzy's warm nature and constant laughter were contagious. As they readied the small wood boxes with s'mores pops inside on the table set aside by the front door so guests could take their gift when they left, Izzy touched a box and sighed. "I just love these."

"I picked up light blue ones so it fit a boy's party," Faith explained.

"Thank you. They look so enticing sitting here. So? Aren't you going to leave your business cards, too? I'm sure you want people to hire you for similar parties."

Faith bit the inside of her cheek. "Of course I do but I didn't want to take advantage. I assumed if you were happy, you would spread the word."

Izzy grinned. "You bet I will. But leave your cards, too." She nudged her gently with her elbow, so Faith dug through her purse and fanned her Sweet Treats cards out on the table beside the party favors.

With a satisfied nod, Izzy led Faith back into the main area of the apartment. "Everyone will be here soon. I have to confess I went a little overboard. There are caterers in the kitchen. But at this age, the kids still come with their parents and I wanted everyone to have good food."

Faith liked the bubbly blonde. She glanced across the room to where Jason stood talking with a tall man with sable hair and dark blue eyes. He had a dominating presence, commanding the room.

"That's my husband, Gabe," Izzy said, following Faith's line of sight. "Come meet him." She took Faith's hand and pulled her across the floor to where the men stood.

After introductions were made, Jason took her off guard by wrapping an arm around her and pulling her against him. "Gabe recommended the private investigator who's looking into your brother," he said quietly.

She nodded, hating the reminder. Although she was living at Jason's, she tried her best not to focus on Colton when she could help it.

"Renault is the best," Gabe said in a soothing tone. "He's also a bodyguard if you need one. It might take time, but he'll locate your sibling." Before they could say more, the doorbell rang at the same time as Noah walked into the room rubbing his eyes.

"Hey, buddy!" Gabe strode over to his son, knelt down, and lifted the little boy into his arms. "It's time for your party."

"Party, yay!" He wriggled to get down just as friends walked into the room and the birthday party began.

Suddenly they were surrounded by children, and

Jason grabbed her hand, pulling her to the side. Parents divided off into groups who knew each other, while Gabe kept a close eye on his son and Izzy flitted from person to person, making sure everyone was happy.

The doorbell rang and a life-size costumed Dalmatian with a red vest and firefighter hat on his head entered the apartment.

He stumbled into the room and the kids yelled and laughed.

"I'm good!" he said as he was surrounded by children.

"Marshall from PAW Patrol," Gabe said, followed by, "I need a drink."

Jason laughed. "I bet you never thought this would be your life," he said to his cousin.

Gabe glared at him. "You have no idea. But … I wouldn't trade it for the world," he said, his voice softening along with his expression as his gaze went from his wife to his little boy, who was sitting on the Dalmatian's lap.

"I'm going to take pictures," Gabe said. He walked over to Izzy, pulled her away from her friends, and wrapped an arm around her while they watched their son interacting with the other kids.

Faith sighed, viewing them, a feeling of longing tugging in her chest.

"What are you thinking?" Jason asked.

She bit the inside of her cheek, uncertain if she wanted to answer with the truth.

"Do you want kids?" he asked before she could answer, upping the stakes with his question to her.

She hesitated before answering. "Not with my life the way it is now, no. Not with a threat looming over me and while I'm still building my business. But someday? Yes. I do." She looked over at him and tossed the hot potato in his lap. "Do you?"

JASON KNEW HE made a mistake the minute he'd asked Faith if she wanted kids. He'd initially meant it as an innocuous question because they'd been surrounded by children, but as soon as it had come out of his mouth, he realized how deep the question was. Her long pause gave his stomach time to twist and turn. And though she had every right to turn the question around on him, she wasn't going to like his answer.

"I don't ... like loss."

She narrowed her gaze, confusion obvious on her face. "But kids don't mean loss."

"Kids mean more people to worry about in my life and that scares me." His heart picked up a rapid beat in his chest, thoughts of Levi taking over, as they always did when he considered a serious future. Which was why he rarely let himself go there.

He glanced at Faith. "Come on."

"Where?"

"Someplace we can talk. We came, we saw, we brought gifts and favors... Izzy and Gabe will understand." As if sensing they were talking about him, Gabe glanced over.

Jason gestured to the door and Gabe nodded, his expression one of understanding. Grasping Faith's hand, he wove through the crowds of people, and they grabbed their coats and slipped out the door. If he was going to have this necessary conversation, he was going to do it in a place that mattered.

"Where are we going?" Faith asked, rushing to keep up with his long strides. He couldn't help it. Thinking about retelling this story made him antsy and anxious and he needed to move.

"You'll see. Just bear with me."

With traffic, it took him thirty minutes to cross town and head up toward the place where he and his *brothers* had met. He pulled onto the city street that housed Manhattan University, where he'd gone to school, and parked in a nearby lot.

"Is this where you, Tanner, Landon, and Levi went to college?" Faith asked after he'd handed the attendant his keys and they started walking up the ramp toward the street.

"What do you know about Levi?" he asked gruffly.

"The night I first met you, I Googled the nightclub and found the website. I read the dedication," she said, her voice soft and full of understanding.

He swallowed over the lump in his throat but remained silent. They walked down the sidewalk and headed along the street known as Fraternity Row and came to a stop at a brownstone with steps leading to the front door. The fraternity located here now was a new one, not the one he and his friends had pledged, but the building was the same, just as the memories remained.

"What happened here?" Faith asked, her hand clasping his.

The bite of the cold wind nipped at his face, but he was here to feel the sensation. Levi wasn't. So he stayed here, as he began to tell Faith the story.

"I met the guys in the dorm. We lived on the same hall and we clicked immediately. The four of us hung out and did everything together. We started school in late August, and of all the guys, I was closest to Levi. We had the same major, business, were in the same classes. He switched to room with me because he wanted a break from his twin." He chuckled at the memory. The guys had started as roommates and things quickly devolved until Levi had wanted out.

"You must get close living together. I went to a

local school, so I wouldn't know. I can only guess," she said.

He nodded. "It's intense." He leaned against the bannister leading up the stairs, and Faith stood beside him. "But it was good until Levi wanted to join a fraternity."

"You didn't?"

Jason shrugged. "I wasn't much of a joiner. I liked doing my own thing. But Levi was persistent. He said the social life would be better, the girls hotter."

"As if any of you had a hard time getting women." Faith's expression was priceless. Shock mixed with disbelief and a healthy dose of sarcasm in her tone.

"Hey. Freshman guys do not get the girls. Trust me."

"If you say so." She lifted one foot, bracing it on a higher step. But she didn't push him for more serious conversation.

Still, he knew it was time. "All the frats had strict rules about alcohol because the drinking age was twenty-one and hazing was strictly forbidden both by school rules and the national fraternity. But why follow the rules, right?" he asked with disgust and obvious pain in his voice.

He didn't even bother to hide it from her nor did he consider it a weakness. No, this event was what defined him and the kind of life he lived. He wasn't embarrassed about hurting because he'd lost his best friend to a stupid, juvenile practice performed by self-righteous, entitled assholes.

Beside him, Faith froze. "Hazing?" She obviously hadn't considered how Levi had died, because she sounded horrified as realization dawned.

"Hazing. A secret practice carried out by older classmen in the basement of this house." Jason gestured with a sweep of his hand toward the building behind them. "Good old-fashioned kissing ass of seniors, doing their bidding, paddling, eating disgusting things I'll spare you from hearing about, and forced alcohol consumption." He clenched his jaw at the memories he did his best to keep far away from his present reality.

"God. Jason, I'm sorry. If you don't want to tell me what happened, I understand." Faith's green eyes were bright with unshed tears as she held on to his hand with hers, her free one in the pocket of her jacket.

The irony didn't escape him and he explained it to her. "I didn't talk about it with anyone. My parents sent me to therapy and I went because they insisted, but I didn't speak. Week after week, I sat in silence until the therapist gave up. So did my parents. They left me to brood. I never wanted to discuss it … until now." He wanted to tell her about the raw pain he'd experienced and then let her soothe the remaining ache.

"Then I'm listening."

He nodded, grateful. "The final initiation, as the upper-class guys called it, was scheduled on a Saturday night. Up until that point, we considered it just bullshit we had to get through to join, but Landon heard rumors that this last party usually got out of hand. And the guys in charge our year were determined to make a name for themselves in the history of the frat. They'd make it more difficult for us than any year before."

Faith squeezed his hand. "Do you want to go inside? Or find someplace warmer to talk?"

"No. I need to do this here." He knew she was cold and he was determined to get through the rest quickly so they could go home and he could lose himself inside her warmth. "We tried to talk Levi out of going but he insisted."

"And you guys weren't going to let him go alone," she correctly guessed.

He nodded. "Right. It started with shots. We could deal with shots of vodka, right? The night passed and we drank. And drank. And soon we were all given handles of what we thought was regular vodka. Turns out it was one hundred proof."

"Crap," she muttered under her breath.

Although he could describe the paddling and the

pain, she didn't need to hear that any more than he needed to relive it. "They insisted we finish a handle. Levi volunteered to go first."

Faith winced but remained silent.

"We told him he didn't have to do it. We each offered to walk out with him and fuck the pledge and the joining, but he was game. He wanted to be accepted so damned badly. So he drank. And drank. Then they put a backpack filled with weights on his back and made him run up and down the basement stairs. He tripped, fell backward, and smacked his head a few times on the way down." Nausea filled his throat at the memory of the sound of his friend's head cracking against the stairs.

Faith wrapped her arms around him as he finished the story, and he took comfort from the warmth of her cheek against his.

"I couldn't call anyone. They'd taken our phones when we arrived and pulled out the landlines ahead of time." He dropped to his knees, remembering his friend lying lifeless on the floor, blood coming from his head, Landon yelling at his brother to wake up, slapping his face in his attempt.

She lowered herself with him, hanging on to him for dear life.

"Then Vic ... Victor Clark, who'd been in charge all along, who put the backpack on Levi and smacked his face when he tripped the first time, called us pussies and demanded we drink next."

"What did you do?"

His eyes burned with unshed tears and his throat was raw from holding them back. "I... We picked up Levi and walked out of the house. Nobody stopped as we headed for the university hospital until finally a campus van picked us up. Levi was DOA."

"Oh, God, Jason, I'm sorry." She clasped her hands against his cheeks and met his gaze. "You all know it wasn't your fault, right?"

He rolled his shoulders. "To this day, I don't fucking know. There are so many ifs. If we hadn't agreed to rush a frat. If we hadn't agreed to go to the party. If we hadn't let him drink and just turned around and went home... But none of it matters because it happened and he's gone. But it's the lesson I took from it that's my point of telling you."

She shivered despite being tight against him. "Which is what?"

"You need to understand. You asked if I wanted kids and I need to explain why I don't. We nearly lost Sienna when she was a kid. I lost Levi. I already have a big family and I have the guys. That's a solid handful of people to worry about already, and I vowed I wouldn't add more." He looked at her, regret all over his handsome face. "I can't have more people who I could potentially lose. Kids? Yeah, that's … more."

✧　✧　✧

FAITH HEARD HIM. She even understood. Her heart broke for what he'd seen and lived through and the pain he still harbored inside him. But what he didn't seem to understand was that he was a warm, giving man who naturally helped people … like her. Which inevitably meant bringing more people into his inner circle. But he didn't want those connections.

He was helping her, yes, but he didn't want to get emotionally involved. If she'd harbored any illusions after their morning in bed, he'd definitely set her straight now. All she could do was to be there for him the way he'd been there for her since the day they'd met.

"Hey." She leaned back and looked into his red-rimmed eyes. "I get it, okay? I understand more than you could imagine. I have a complicated life that doesn't lend toward bringing people in. My brother is dangerous. By letting anyone in, I put them in danger, too. I never wanted to do that to you but you insisted. So the truth is, I get needing to keep people at a distance."

He remained silent, as if sensing she wasn't finished. Which she wasn't.

She drew a deep breath and continued. "So if

you're worried about me wanting anything more from you than the help you're offering now, I won't. I don't."

Relief crossed his face even as the word *lies* echoed inside her head. Of course she wanted more than he could give, because she'd fallen for her reluctant hero. But that wasn't in the cards. She'd deal with her pain like she dealt with everything else, by throwing herself into her work and building her business.

She just needed to convince Jason he could trust her to respect his boundaries. "My plan is for my brother to end up in jail so I can go back to living my independent life." She forced a smile. "We're good, Jason. *You're* good. Most importantly, you survived. Don't feel guilty because you did."

He squeezed her hand and rose to his feet, then together they headed back to the car.

Chapter Seven

FAITH TOOK HER cues from Jason, who was silent on the way home after the trip to the frat house. She gave him his space, not wanting to intrude on his personal thoughts, using the time to check in with Kelsey, who had everything at the store under control. She even offered to open in the morning, and since she knew the recipes and they had nonperishable items to sell, Faith agreed.

She realized, however, it was time to hire more people to help at the store. Not only because of the Colton situation and the fact that she couldn't always be there right now, but because she deserved some time off. She'd been handling things by herself for a year, with only Kelsey part-time to help out. So that was on her definite to-do list and ASAP.

Jason had been so quiet, even on the elevator ride up to his apartment, that it took her by surprise when, after they entered the apartment, took off their jackets, and hung them in the closet, he spun her around, pulling her against him.

"I need you," he said, and she had no intention of denying him. Not after how he'd bared his soul to her earlier, helping her to understand everything about him.

She kicked off her shoes and socks, lifted her hands and unbuttoned each button, letting her shirt drop to the floor. His heated stare fell to her full breasts, and as he watched, she reached behind her and released the bra clasp, letting the straps fall down her arms. Cool air rushed over her nipples, hardening them into tight peaks.

Feeling his gaze hot on hers, she unbuttoned her trousers, releasing them as well. She kicked the pants aside.

Jason's eyes darkened with need. "Go on."

She swallowed hard. Hooking her fingers into her panties, she pulled them down and off, leaving her standing in the entryway of his apartment naked. She stared at him. His hooded gaze, the flush in his cheeks peeking over the scruff on his face, and the fact that he was fully dressed all worked to arouse her unbearably. Dampness slickened between her thighs and her sex throbbed with desire. But she was well aware that this was Jason's show, his pace, his pain that he needed to work out.

As she stood bared to him, he removed his shoes. His socks, shirt, and slacks along with his boxer briefs came next, tossed onto the pile of her clothes. His erection stood prominently against his belly, the sight causing a throbbing in her core.

She licked her lips and his eyes darkened at the sight.

Slowly, she stepped closer to him, her gaze never leaving his, then she lowered herself to her knees.

"Faith," he said, a harsh warning in his tone.

She looked up at him through her lashes and smiled. "Yes?"

"Fuck," he said, his hand coming to rest on her head.

He needed this, that much she knew, and if she could make him forget his troubles for a little while, that's what she wanted to do. Because she was coming to care deeply for this dark knight of hers.

She wrapped her hand around his stiffness, gliding her palm over the velvety yet rigid length. Dipping her head, she licked the salty white coating off the head and he groaned, his fingers tightening in her hair. The tug was arousing, turning her on, but not as much as being on her knees and giving him pleasure. And that was her goal.

With her hand on the base of his shaft, she opened her mouth and glided her lips down his cock. His big body shuddered and she grew heady with the knowledge that she affected him. Pulling him inside her mouth, she slicked her tongue over and under his thick member. She drew him deep until the head of his cock hit the back of her throat. Forcing herself to relax, she swallowed over him, managing not to choke, and he yanked harder on her hair.

She groaned around him as he began to rock his hips back and forth, thrusting his cock into her mouth, using her to take what he needed. With her hands now braced on his thighs, she let him take over. He pumped himself in and out, and she sucked him harder, causing a warning tap on her head.

"I'm going to come," he said gruffly, clearly expecting her to release him, but she had other plans.

She hummed around him and urged him to continue. He thrust once, twice, and came with a grunt, streaming down her throat, and she swallowed over and over until he relaxed, sliding out of her mouth.

"Shit, sweetness, I wanted that to be inside you."

"It was," she said with a pleased chuckle. He helped her to her feet and, taking her off guard, lifted her into his arms. She squeaked in surprise and wrapped her arms around his neck, as he carried her into his bedroom.

No sooner had he deposited her on the bed than he spread her thighs and came down over her, his face level with her sex, and began to lick, suck, and devour her like a starving man. At the first slide of his tongue, she moaned, suddenly aware of how very aroused she already was.

His mouth worked magic, the experience fresh and new, as everything with Jason seemed to be. He knew his way around her body. She'd never known her breasts were sensitive, never realized she could come from oral sex. But as he slid his tongue inside her, his nose nudging her clit, waves of sensation and aware-ness shuddered through her. Warm and delicious, her body responded to his intense ministrations, the way he delicately played with her clit causing her to buck against him.

He must have realized he'd hit the right spot, be-cause he pulled the tight bud into his mouth and grazed it with his teeth. A swell of desire took hold and didn't let go as he brought her up and over the edge.

She'd been grasping the comforter, hanging on as he ate at her, but with the surge of desire, she needed to hold on to him. She grasped his hand as she ground her sex against his mouth, riding out the most explo-sive climax she'd ever had.

Before she could fully finish, he'd come over her, nudging her legs apart and pushing himself deep.

"Oh, God, Jason!" She quivered around him, her inner walls clasping him harder. "I'm coming again."

"Damn right you are," he muttered and slammed

into her, grinding his hips against her.

She whimpered at the assault, his body rough with hers in all the best possible ways. Her gaze on his as she came, she fell into those dark blue eyes, losing herself in this man who'd all but sworn he would never truly be hers.

Pushing those thoughts aside, she let her body enjoy the peak and slow tumble back to reality, coming to with his big body on top of hers. With a grunt, he rolled to his side, pulling out of her, and she felt the loss in more ways than physical.

He pressed a long kiss on her lips. "Be right back," he said and rose to walk into the bathroom. She heard the water run, and he returned, helping her clean up before pulling her back into his arms.

They dozed for a while, and when she woke up, he was staring into her eyes. "Thank you," he said in a gruff voice.

"For what?"

"Letting me take what I needed. Giving me more than I deserve."

She lay her head in the crook of his shoulder. "You carry a lot of pain inside you. It's good to let it out."

He merely grunted in reply.

"I have a question," she said, having realized earlier that this was the one thing he hadn't addressed.

His arm pulled her tighter against him. "What's

that?"

Drawing a deep breath, she asked, "Who's the woman and the little boy in the picture on your desk?"

He exhaled slowly. "When Levi died, he had a girlfriend, Amber. He didn't know it at the time but he'd gotten her pregnant."

"Oh, God."

She felt him nod. "Yeah."

"In the beginning, there wasn't much the guys and I could do but be there for her, but after the club started bringing in money, we helped her out. LJ, that's his name, Levi Jr., means a lot to all of us."

"That's so sad," she whispered, unable to imagine how difficult the woman's life had been. A single mother, still in college…

"She doesn't live in the city, so we don't see them nearly as much as we'd like, but the relationship is strong."

And LJ was the child he already had, Faith realized, her heart pounding hard in her chest at the thought. These men and the bond they shared with each other, and with Amber and her son, gave Jason all the family he believed he needed.

They lay in silence, each lost in their own thoughts. After today, Faith understood Jason more than ever. She'd never felt so close to him … and he'd never felt further out of reach.

✧ ✧ ✧

THE NEXT MORNING, Jason woke up before Faith. Last night, they'd stayed up late, ordered in pizza, and ... dammit, he couldn't call it having sex. He'd made love to her.

After the hard, punishing way he'd taken her the first time, they'd fallen asleep again, and then he'd found himself sliding into her slowly. Rocking against her as she woke up to him pumping in and out of her, their gazes locked on each other, emotions passing between them. Despite his vow to remain detached, he hadn't been able to do it. Not with this woman who was burrowing her way deep inside him.

Not that it changed anything. When her problems were solved, she'd go back to her life and he'd return to his. Solitary and safe, the way he liked it. He had no choice. He didn't see himself opening up enough for marriage and a family, and that's what Faith wanted. What she deserved.

He muttered a curse, and leaving her sleeping, he slipped out of bed. He pulled on a pair of sweats before walking to the kitchen, where he immediately made himself a cup of coffee. Yesterday had been unexpected and brutal, the revelation of his past completely unplanned, but if there was anyone he would share his pain with, it would be Faith.

Somehow they'd bonded, and he trusted her as much as his brothers, which was odd. And something that unnerved him to no end. Also something he didn't want to think about too much, so he picked up his coffee mug, drank his caffeine, and began scrolling through his phone, checking in on Landon and Tanner.

Jason had missed a Saturday night at the club, and his partners weren't pissed exactly, but they weren't happy with him, either. Since there was no way he was going to tell them he'd been reliving their shared past, he let them give him shit and took it as his due.

He'd finished his first cup of coffee and was on his standard second when his doorbell rang, startling him. He narrowed his gaze.

He glanced at his phone. Eleven a.m. Who would be here at this early hour on a Sunday? He strode to the door, glanced in the peephole, and did a double take.

Unsetting his alarm, he unlocked the door and swung it open. "Mom? What in the world are you doing here?"

Savannah Dare walked into his apartment, but instead of the tears he expected, he saw anger in her blue eyes. "Your father wants me back. Of all the self-centered, ridiculous notions, he thinks I'm going to forgive and forget." She met Jason's gaze and pulled him into her arms. "I'm sorry. How's my boy?" she asked, hugging him tight. She smelled like the perfume he associated with home, a light floral scent that said *mom*.

"I'm fine. And we'll talk about Dad. But why are you *here*?"

"He showed up last night with his flowers and apologies and I told him to leave. He swore he'd be back this morning. I wasn't ready to deal with him, so I left."

"The state? Why didn't you just go stay with Alex and Madison?" he asked of his brother and sister-in-law, who lived nearby his mom.

"That's the first place your father would look for me. And with the baby, I didn't want to just show up on Sienna's doorstep." She rolled her suitcase into the entryway and met his gaze. "Show me to your guest room?"

Jason rubbed a hand over his face, wondering how he was going to explain away the fact that he had a woman staying in the extra room who was currently fast asleep in his bed.

"Jason?" As if on cue, Faith walked into the living area wearing nothing but his shirt from last night, buttoned and hanging down on her bare thighs. Her gaze landed on his mother and her eyes opened wide. "Oh my God. You have company!" She pulled at the shirt as if she could magically lengthen the fabric.

"Jason Dare, why didn't you tell me you had a woman here?" his mother asked in a chiding voice.

"I was just about to," he muttered. And though he was a grown man and had every right to have a woman in his bed, he wasn't thrilled that Faith's face had turned beet red and she looked mortified.

He had no choice but to introduce them. "Mom, this is Faith Lancaster. Faith, this is my mother, Savannah Dare."

He gave Faith credit. Despite her embarrassment, she walked right up to his mom, extended her hand, and said, "It's nice to meet you."

"The same here. I apologize for interrupting. I flew in from Florida unannounced. I'll just go–"

"No. I, umm … I'll go get dressed and let you two talk." Faith turned and fled back the way she'd come.

With a groan, he glanced at his mother. "That went well."

She tucked a strand of her blonde hair behind her ear. "I'm really sorry. I should have called but I just took the six-a.m. flight."

"It's fine. It's just that the situation with Faith is complicated. She's staying here because she has some personal issues right now and despite her … being in my shirt, she's using the spare bedroom," he said instead of saying *despite the obvious fact that we're sleeping together.* It was awkward enough for everyone.

His mother nodded in understanding. "I didn't stay in a hotel because your father has contacts and private investigators. He'll track me down. At least this way, once he finds me, he has to deal with us both. But given the circumstances, I can take a room. Or go stay with Sienna. I can help with the baby. I just didn't want to intrude because they're still newlyweds, but it's really no problem." She was rambling.

"No." Faith returned, dressed in a pair of jeans and a tee shirt, her hair brushed and pulled into a sleek ponytail. "I can go home. You stay here with your son."

"Not happening, Faith, and you know why." Jason's words came out like a command and had her snapping her shoulders back and narrowing her gaze.

"I'm not putting your mother out. It's not right."

Savannah looked from Jason to Faith, following the conversation although obviously not understanding the reasons behind their argument.

"Then you can stay in my room and my mother can take the guest room," Jason said. "Unless you want to go home and be a sitting duck for Colton to find you?" He folded his arms across his chest, daring her to challenge him.

Faith's shoulders, the evidence of her strength and defiance seconds before, wilted as he made his point.

"Okay. Thank you. I realize I'm putting everyone out, but you're right. I have nowhere else to go." Her hands came up to her neck as she obviously remembered being hurt by her brother.

He hated having had to bring up those memories in order to get his way and keep her safe.

"Obviously the person who should go to a hotel is me," his mother said when they'd both gone silent.

"No," Faith and Jason said at once. They both knew they were sleeping together. The chances of him letting her go back to her own bed while she was under his roof were slim to none anyway. He wanted to get his fill of her while he could.

He ignored the voice in his head telling him he'd never have enough of her and faced his mother. "Looks like you're staying."

"Okay." His mother smiled at them both.

Faith smiled back. "I'll go pack up my things and move them into your room," she said, her cheeks only slightly red at this point.

"Great. Now that that's settled, Mom, come in, take off your coat, and make yourself at home." He met Faith's gaze, shooting her a grateful look he hoped she could translate, along with an apologetic one.

This was a turn of events he'd never expected, having his mother and his ... Faith, under one roof. And he had no idea how to handle the situation.

✧ ✧ ✧

AN HOUR AFTER Jason's mother arrived, Faith found herself at an upscale restaurant, sitting next to Jason and across the table from Savannah Dare. She was a lovely woman with blonde hair and light blue eyes, a warm smile, and an easy air of acceptance of having found Faith all but in her son's bed.

Once Faith had recovered from her embarrassment and accepted the fact that she really had nowhere else to go if she wanted to be safe, she realized she'd have to move into Jason's room. His mother seemed to handle it easily enough.

Savannah drank a mimosa, Jason and Faith coffee, and after the waiter took their orders, Jason glanced at his mother. "So Dad wants you back?"

Faith held back a shocked sound.

Savannah looked to Faith.

"She knows," Jason said. "I told her everything about my family situation."

Savannah raised her eyebrows, obviously surprised her son had opened up. But she nodded her head and launched into her story. "Before Robert ran off to Barbados with his mistress, he told me he wanted a divorce. For reasons I can't fathom, he's returned with a change of heart. He wants me back."

Jason grimaced and Faith knew what he thought of

146

that idea.

"And what do you want?" he asked his mother, to his credit not giving his own verbal input. Yet.

Savannah lifted the glass and took a sip of her drink. "I had already resigned myself to a divorce, but more than that, your father's behavior forced me to take a good look at my past." She glanced down at her plate. "I might not have known he was married when we met, but when I found out, I didn't leave him. That makes me complicit."

Faith squirmed in her seat, but Savannah seemed comfortable enough talking about personal issues in front of her.

"Mom—"

"No. It's true. I justified it by telling myself his marriage to Emma hadn't been for love, but that doesn't make what I did right. The truth is, the man is a cheater. If I take him back, he's bound to do it again. It isn't like it's only happened once, after all."

Jason nodded in agreement. "I hate to admit that you're right because he's my father … but you are. And as long as you're saying these things yourself, I can say I agree with you and your decision."

Listening to mother and son, Faith marveled at a few things. One, how close they obviously were, but then Jason had said his family was everything to him. Two, the burden he carried on his shoulders. A father he couldn't look up to, a mother he obviously loved and wanted to take care of, and a past of his own that was heavy and painful. No wonder he didn't want to add any more people to his responsibilities.

"Faith, honey, I'm so sorry to put you in the middle of listening to my problems." The sound of her name shook Faith out of her musings.

"It's no problem, Mrs. Dare. I'm really the intruder here."

"First, call me Savannah, and second, nonsense. Now tell me how you and my son met."

Faith bit the inside of her cheek, then said, "He rescued me when I was stuck with a flat tire one night and somehow has become entangled in my problems."

Savannah nodded somberly. "Yes, he told me about those issues while you were showering and getting ready. Money does such dreadful things to people. Really. I'm sorry about your brother."

"Well, he had a drug problem long before my mother passed away and left me a small inheritance. The fact that there was money just makes it all worse. It gives him a reason to come after me. I just can't believe he's been able to stay under the radar for so long." She shifted in her seat, automatically looking out the window. As if her brother would magically appear, but of course he didn't.

Jason frowned at the reminder of Colton. "He's

hanging out with people who have no way of being found. Other addicts and dealers, probably. But I have faith in Jack Renault." He looked to his mother. "That's the PI Gabe recommended."

Savannah nodded, then reached over and took Faith's hand. "My son is a good man. He's solid and dependable. I am sure he'll see to it your situation is resolved and you're safe." She squeezed once before letting go.

"Thank you," Faith whispered.

To her surprise, at that motherly gesture and those kind, reassuring words, a lump rose to her throat. Savannah Dare reminded Faith of her own mom, and the loss she still felt deeply, even if she was often too busy to dwell on her pain.

Jason looked from his mother to Faith, a furrow between his brows, a somber look on his handsome face. Although up to now, she'd learned to read him fairly well, she had no idea what was going on behind the masked expression he wore. But if she had to guess, something about having his mother and Faith together, getting to know one another, was throwing him for a loop.

He wouldn't want Faith to get attached. To feel like she belonged with them. And she wouldn't, she promised herself. She'd do her best to put an emotional wall up against the motherly gestures and the

sweetness that came from Savannah and not miscon-
strue Jason's protectiveness for anything more. At the
end of the road, she had herself. And no one else.

✧   ✧   ✧

LATER THAT EVENING, Jason escaped to the bedroom,
leaving his mother and Faith alone in the kitchen,
discussing candy making and other things. He needed
a break from the emotional drama that was his mother
and father, and he needed to step back from his
intense feelings for Faith. He hadn't forgotten the
night they'd just spent together or the way he feared
she was cracking his heart open, exposing him to
potential pain. The pain that always came from loving
someone and the possibility of loss that came with it.

Sitting down on the bed, he picked up his cell and
called his brother, who answered on the first ring.

"Jason," Alex said. "Good to hear from you."

"Hey, man. How are you, Madison, and the kid-
let?"

"All great. What's up?"

Jason blew out a long breath. No point beating
around the bush. "I've got company. Mom's here."

"What?" Alex asked, startled. "She didn't tell me
she was leaving town," he said, confusion in his voice.

"Well, apparently it wasn't a planned trip. She was
running away." Jason drummed his fingers on the

nightstand.

"From Dad."

"You got it," he muttered. "He returned from wherever he was and decided he wants her back. She, on the other hand, has come to terms with the man he is and is ready to move on. But she didn't want to deal with him yet, so she's here."

"Damn. I'm sorry it landed on your lap."

Jason shrugged. "It's fine. It's Mom. She's always welcome. I just figured you didn't know yet and wanted to give you a heads-up in case Dad comes sniffing around your place looking for her."

Alex let out a low growl. "I'll deal with him. What about Sienna?"

"Mom called her earlier today. She's going to see her in the morning. Mom stopped by a baby store and loaded up on things for Lizzy. I have a feeling Sienna will beg her to stay there and help out, but she's welcome here for as long as she needs."

Jason didn't mention Faith to his brother. He didn't feel like getting into the situation he'd found himself in. In fact, he thought, he was actually ready to crash. He needed a good night's sleep.

"Well, tell Mom I say hi and to call me if she needs me. And don't worry. I'll handle Dad if he shows up here."

"Thanks," Jason said. "Talk to you soon." He disconnected the phone, but before he could go to sleep, he had another call to make.

He scrolled through his contacts and dialed his brother-in-law, the famous musician with Tangled Royal, now a songwriter, Grey Kingston.

"Jason?" Grey answered quickly. "How's things in New York?"

"All good. You and Avery?" he asked of his half sister.

"We're fine, too. So what can I do for you?"

Jason chuckled. That was Grey, right to the point. He leaned back against the headboard and stretched out his legs. "Well, the guys and I are expanding what we do at the club. We want to bring in live entertainment and launch with a big name." He drew a deep breath. "We were thinking of you."

Grey paused before answering. "I'm honored you want me. But you know I haven't been singing publicly anymore. I'm more of a songwriter than an entertainer these days. Hang on."

Jason heard noise and then, "I'm on the phone with your brother Jason, sugar. You feeling okay?"

Whatever Avery said was muffled and Jason couldn't hear.

"I'm back," Grey said. "So about the club."

Jason crossed his fingers. "We figured your absence from the stage would make you more of a draw now. A limited appearance, if you will." He knew he was asking a lot of Grey, but he hoped the other man was itching to play in public once more.

Grey chuckled. "It's not that I couldn't be persuaded, but there are things going on here…"

"It's okay. Tell him," Jason heard Avery say.

He narrowed his gaze. "Is everything really okay there?" He was suddenly worried.

"Yes. It's just that Avery's pregnant and it's been a little difficult these first few months. I don't want to leave her to perform," Grey explained. "We haven't told anyone yet, so if you could keep it quiet until we're ready to let the family know, we'd appreciate it."

"No problem." A wave of happiness took hold of Jason along with concern for Avery. Still, Grey had given him good news. "Congratulations! And give Avery a kiss for me. No worries. I'll find someone else to play," Jason assured him, glad Avery had a man who was so devoted to her.

"When are you thinking about doing the first gig? I'll make some calls and see if I can get you someone solid," Grey said.

Jason winced as he answered. "Within the next few weeks. I know it's short notice—"

Grey let out a low whistle. "No kidding. But let me see what I can do."

"Thanks." They said their goodbyes, and then Jason spoke to Avery for a few minutes, congratulating her and reassuring himself that she was suffering from severe morning sickness and nothing more serious.

He disconnected the call as Faith walked into the room and shut the door behind her. She looked adorable in a pair of curve-hugging leggings with white stripes down the side and a white tee shirt that showcased her delectable breasts. Despite it all, his body reacted to hers. He wanted her. He had a feeling he'd always want her.

"Hi. Everything okay?" she asked, gesturing to the phone he still held in his hand.

He nodded. "Avery is pregnant. My half sister," he explained, a smile on his face.

"That's great news!" Faith lowered herself to the bed, sitting beside him.

"It is." Another Dare baby. More people to add to those he loved and worried about, he thought. "What's doing with my mom?"

"She turned in for the night. I think the long day finally caught up with her."

He nodded. "Did she mention my father?"

Faith shook her head. "I got the distinct impression she didn't want to go there. We talked about other things. I like her." She studied him intently, her brows furrowed over narrowed eyes. "What's wrong?"

She was exceptionally good at reading him, he

thought. But he wasn't up for an emotional conversation tonight. Especially when he had no idea what he wanted to reveal about his feelings.

"I'm just tired. I think I'll take a shower and turn in early, too," he said.

She flinched at his brusque tone. But for a man used to living alone, to thriving on being by himself, he found himself suddenly surrounded by women. By emotions. Theirs as well as his. And though he wanted to lose himself in her body, he was afraid that meant losing his heart as well. And he wasn't ready to face that truth. Not now.

And maybe not ever.

Chapter Eight

JASON FINISHED HIS cup of coffee and glanced at the two women looking at him expectantly. He turned to his mother first. "I'm going to drop you off at Sienna's on my way to work." He'd been neglecting his duties, and one of the things he'd decided while tossing and turning last night was that it was time for him to get back to normal. To do his job while protecting Faith at the same time.

The new arrangement would also allow him to get his bearings and his emotions back on an even keel. They'd been together twenty-four seven, and it was messing with what he knew he both wanted and needed in his life.

He met Faith's curious gaze, and he knew she was going to be hurt by what he said next. Gritting his teeth, he dove in. "I called Jack Renault, and he's going to pick you up and escort you to work today. He'll be on bodyguard duty, so you have nothing to worry about."

He'd caught her, mug halfway to her mouth. She

slowly lowered it and nodded. She met his gaze, to her credit, not looking away as he severed the routine they'd been in for the last few weeks with no explanation.

"Okay." She straightened her shoulders, clearly holding back whatever she was feeling. "What time will he be here?"

"Thirty minutes."

She nodded. "I'm going to finish getting ready." She placed the mug into the sink, and without another word, she turned and walked away.

Jason exhaled, watching her go.

"What did you just do?" his mother asked in the tone he recognized as the chiding one from when he was a child.

He ran a hand over his face before answering. "What do you mean?"

"Don't play dumb with me, Jason. I spent last night with Faith. I know you've been working from her shop, protecting her, making sure she's safe. Now suddenly you're sending her with a bodyguard? The poor girl looked blindsided."

He swallowed back a curse. He probably could have handled it better. But when? He'd made the call to Renault while she showered, then fallen asleep on his side of the bed before she'd turned in for the night. He just needed a break and he took it. He left her in bed to shower and later met up with her in the kitchen.

"It's for the best," he told his mother. "We were getting too attached. It wasn't a normal situation. The guys were getting annoyed that I wasn't there. We're close to opening a new version of the club. I need to be focused."

She narrowed her gaze. "What did it?" she asked, lowering her voice. "Was it your father? Me? Almost losing Sienna? Or was it Levi that severed you emotionally?"

He reared back in shock. All this time he'd thought he'd kept his feelings to himself. Gone about his life. Lived it to the fullest. He never showed anyone his weakness, and yet here was his mother, nailing it in one breath.

"All of it maybe?" he said, uncharacteristically allowing himself to have this conversation.

"Jason, I can see how deeply you care about this woman. She's special. She's intelligent, smart, can run a business, and she cares about you. Don't lose her because you're afraid."

He shook his head. It went so much deeper than that. He didn't deserve happiness when Levi was buried and he'd done nothing to stop it. This was a thought he rarely let himself have, but he allowed it now because he needed the reminder. With his mother pushing him toward Faith and Faith's pull so strong, he had to prompt his memory. The thought of Levi would keep him strong when desire threatened to pull him into the light.

"I can't, Mom. She deserves someone who can give her everything. And I've given up on having it all." He deliberately glanced at the clock on the microwave. "We need to get going."

Savannah Dare sighed. "One day you're going to look back and realize that you alone destroyed any chance you had at happiness. A chance you deserved. And one Levi would want you to have and live for him."

He shook his head and walked away.

✧   ✧   ✧

JACK RENAULT WAS a large man, bulky and heavyset, wearing a blazer beneath his winter jacket. Faith felt safe with him but not as safe as she'd been knowing Jason was nearby. She wasn't stupid. She knew their arrangement couldn't last. Not when he had an important business to run that had opposite hours of her own, but she'd enjoyed the time she had with him.

And if she'd given it thought, she'd have assumed they'd have an adult conversation before he up and hired a bodyguard and went back to his normal routine. Instead he'd waited until he'd slept with her and then run scared. She had no doubt that's what had occurred, either.

After an incredible night where he'd opened up emotionally, after they'd given themselves to each other in intimate ways she'd never have imagined, he'd slipped out of bed before her and she'd woken up alone. She had no doubt it had been deliberate. Then his mother had arrived and they'd had no time alone to rehash or discuss, and she honestly thought Jason was relieved. Now she had a bodyguard and Jason's distance spoke volumes.

Well, it wasn't like she had nothing to do. Although it had only been this past weekend that she'd provided the treats for Izzy's son's birthday, three of her friends had contacted her via email already.

"Faith?" Kelsey called her from the kitchen.

"Yes?" She glanced out at the shop devoid of customers and walked into the back.

The young woman seemed nervous, which was unlike her.

"What's up?" Faith asked.

"I was wondering if you had more hours for me? My classes this semester are almost over and I–"

"Yes!" Faith didn't even let her finish. "Yes, of course. As a matter of fact, I was thinking of hiring someone else, as well. It'll free me up for other parts of the business," she said, and went on to explain the party favor aspect she'd discovered courtesy of Izzy Dare. "I want to build the business and you're going to be a key part."

Kelsey's eyes lit up at the prospect. "I won't let you down," she promised.

And Faith didn't think she would.

Kelsey returned to work, and Faith headed back out front, her gaze falling on Jack Renault, who looked fierce as his stare held the front door.

She sighed. If this mess didn't end soon, she wouldn't have customers. Jack Renault's expression would scare them off.

Faith walked up to him, meeting his gaze. "Can we talk?"

"What can I do for you, Ms. Lancaster?"

"I want to know why it's been so hard to find my brother? And if we do find him, how can we prove he's been vandalizing my business and my house? I need to get my life back!" And so did Jason.

He'd made it clear he was finished giving up his time for her, and she wanted to free him up and get out of his space. As much as it hurt her heart, because she was definitely falling for the man, he couldn't give her what she wanted or needed. Oh, when he'd made love to her, she'd believed it, but not when he'd shut her out right after.

"Your brother is obviously hanging out with people who aren't on the radar, so to speak. I haven't been able to track a cell. He's gone underground."

She frowned, wrapping her arms around herself. "What if I lure him out somehow?"

Now it was the other man's turn to scowl. "Look, I don't know how you'd find him, for one thing, and for another, Jason Dare wouldn't just fire and not pay me, he'd have my head on a platter. Then Gabriel Dare would let me go and that's my bread and butter. So I suggest you stay put. Your brother's going to mess up sooner or later and we'll get him. I'm pretty damn sure it'll be illegal, which will put him in jail. Just relax and let me do my job. You go make candy," he said, talking down to her, which she didn't appreciate.

Stamping her feet wouldn't help, so she spun around and headed back behind the counter. She couldn't give Jason his space if she wasn't safe, and she couldn't change the status quo, either. Which left her frustrated at having to wait for Colton to make a move.

✧　✧　✧

JASON SPENT THE day and night at the club, back on his usual schedule. In an odd way, his mother's issues had allowed him to take a step back from Faith. After spending the day with Sienna, his mom was at his apartment with Faith, both women being watched over by Jack Renault's nighttime bodyguard outside the building, who would keep both Colton and Robert Dare far away.

Jason didn't have to worry about either of them. He was free to do his job. It was exactly what he'd wanted ... so why was he so fucking stir-crazy and unable to concentrate on anything but what Faith was doing? Worse, what Faith was feeling after his dick move of dumping her on a bodyguard with no warning.

"Hey, where do we stand with entertainment?" Landon asked, walking into Jason's office, where he'd been holed up all day. Normally they sat together in the joint space, but Jason hadn't been in the mood for the ribbing he'd take about finally joining them again.

"Grey's out. My half sister's pregnant and not feeling well," he said, knowing it wasn't like Landon was going to spill the beans to Jason's family. "He's trying to get us a performer."

"Have you reached out to Charlotte as a possibility?" Tanner walked into the room, a can of cola in his hand.

Jason groaned and closed his eyes, a picture of Charlotte, her long black hair and willowy body, filtering through his brain. Worse, the memory of her hands on his body as they'd fucked also made its way through. He didn't want anyone touching him but

Faith. Shit.

He shook his head. "Anyone but her," he muttered.

Tanner narrowed his gaze. "Are you really that far gone for the girl that you can't even hire an ex to sing?"

Yes. "No. I just don't want to deal with her wandering hands and inability to take no for an answer. It took me long enough to convince her it was over last time. No need to go there again."

One stalker in a family was enough, he mused, thinking of Faith's brother, until his words caught him up short. Family? Faith?

He groaned and ran a hand through his hair. "Can you assholes leave? I'm trying to get work done. You left me spreadsheets and work up the ass."

Landon shook his head and laughed, while Tanner said what he was thinking. "Whipped, man. Let me know when the wedding is."

Jason balled up a sheet of paper and tossed it at his friends. Then he went back to work. He wanted to finish up the paperwork before the club got busy for the night. It would be the first time he was downstairs in weeks, and he needed to put on a good show for his partners that everything was fine and back to normal.

An hour later, he'd reconciled some deliveries, made sure everything was copacetic, and was ready to join Landon and Tanner at the bar when his phone rang.

A glance told him it was Grey. Hope sprung in his veins. "Hey," he said, answering immediately.

"Hi. Listen, I tried. All the A-listers are booked every weekend for the next month. Even asking for favors didn't work. Now I can get you Lola," he said of Lola Corbin.

Now Lola Grissom, married to Rep Grissom Jr., a Major League Baseball player, she was the former lead singer of Tangled Royal when Grey's band had been together.

"But I have bad news," Grey said.

A tingle raced up Jason's spine and he almost guessed the information, but he let Grey tell him anyway. "She's been working with Charlotte Jasper, who was with her when I asked … and they both want to do the gig."

"Motherfucker." But he couldn't deny the fact that both Lola and Charlotte together would put Club TEN29 on the map when it came to live acts. It would prove their cachet, and other stars would be willing to sign on to sing here. He let out another groan. "I'll get my attorney to send them a contract and we'll negotiate from there."

"Sorry, man."

"No, I should be thanking you. No worries. How's

Avery?" he asked.

"In the fucking bathroom puking. I don't know how women do it or why they call it *morning* sickness," Grey said, his admiration and worry for his wife obvious.

"Give her my love. I'm going to make the arrangements." Jason disconnected and immediately texted his partners the news.

He then called his attorney and after that he called Gabe. Stars like Lola and Charlotte together were going to cost a mint and they'd need a loan until they were earning back what they paid on the talent.

Finally, he headed down to the darkness that was his bar. A place he'd always loved, but now he couldn't wait to get home.

✧　　✧　　✧

"ARE YOU SURE this is a good idea?" Faith asked Savannah Dare, who was eyeing the dresses she'd had delivered from a personal shopper at Neiman Marcus.

"I think it's the best idea I've had in a long time. We're going to visit my son at his nightclub. We're going to have a few drinks, have a night out, and enjoy." Savannah picked up an emerald-colored garment lying on the bed. "This one is for you. I had three sent over, but the green matches your eyes."

Faith lifted the beautiful garment and draped it

over her arm.

"Don't forget the shoes." Savannah pointed to a pair of silver strap sandals. "Those are your size."

Wondering how she'd allowed the woman to talk her into this, Faith headed for Jason's bathroom, where she'd moved her makeup. Thirty minutes later, the women met up in the family room, dressed to kill. Or be killed, when Jason laid eyes on them outside of the apartment, Faith thought.

"He's going to be so mad," she muttered as Savannah, wearing a silver dress, opened the door to the apartment.

"That big bodyguard will be with us. He'll get over it. I haven't had a night out to just enjoy myself in God knows how long. I'm going. Are you with me?" Jason's mother asked.

Faith picked up the small purse Savannah had also had delivered. "Let's go." She hadn't had any time out in over a year. If anyone was overdue, she was. Jason was obviously working out his own issues, but that didn't mean she couldn't let loose for once.

And Savannah was right. They had a bodyguard. Let Jason be angry. He was the one who'd hired the man, so he must trust him, she thought, as the apartment door slammed closed behind them with a final thud.

✧ ✧ ✧

WITH A SELTZER over ice in hand, Jason made the rounds of the *important* people, those who paid a hefty sum to get into the nightclub and be guaranteed a private table and server. As the manager, it was his job to ensure everyone's happiness at his establishment, and Tanner and Landon had been handling things in his absence.

It felt good to be back in the swing of things and pick up his routine. Apparently his partners felt the same, because from the other side of the room, Tanner raised a glass to Jason, and he did the same.

The other man strode across the room and came up to where Jason stood on the raised balcony area, where Jason had come for a break. "Welcome back, buddy. Good to have you here."

"Thanks. Good to be here." He slid his gaze toward the front entrance just in time to see two women walk into the room. Women he'd recognize in his sleep.

His *mother*, in a silver sequined dress and matching heels, her blonde hair curling around her face in the style she preferred, looked around, taking in her surroundings. She'd been here for the grand opening and so she already had her bearings.

The second woman didn't have the same air of

confidence, but with her rocking body, she didn't need to. The emerald-green dress hugged her curves, the dip in the front revealing cleavage he felt extremely possessive over, and the way it draped her hips and ended above her knees was fucking sexy.

Neither one of them belonged here. He didn't care if the big bodyguard he'd hired trailed close behind.

"Hold this," he said to Tanner, who'd muttered, "Oh, shit," at the same time.

"I'm not missing this," his partner said and followed him through the back curtain and down the stairs.

He stood unnoticed for now at the bar, where he heard his mother order a gin and tonic for herself. Faith was looking at the drink menu, then whispered something in his mother's ear.

"A ménage à trois for my friend," Savannah said with a grin.

Jason closed his eyes and shook his head. He and his partners knew how to make every drink on the menu, and this one included crushed strawberries, fresh basil, white rum, triple sec, lemon juice, Gomme syrup, and ice, mixed then strained. They could be potent and Faith, despite her obvious nerves – she kept licking and biting on her pink-coated lips – had trouble written all over her tonight.

He let her take a sip, which translated into too big

a gulp, before he decided to show himself.

"Hello, ladies," he said, walking over to them, which they had to know was inevitable.

"Jason!" Faith's exclamation was real.

"Hello, son." His mother waggled her fingers at him, clearly pleased with herself.

"And what are you drinking tonight?" he asked politely, even though he knew. He wanted to watch Faith squirm.

Behind him, Tanner chuckled.

"A gin and tonic. You know my drink of choice." His mother shot him a smile and took a delicate sip.

"Faith? What is that in your glass?" Jason asked.

Her cheeks flamed a bright red. "A ménage à trois. Want one?" she asked, finding her cheekiness despite her embarrassment.

"How about you finish your drinks and head home, where it's safe?" he suggested, keeping his anger in check. He'd left them protected. Yet here they were.

Faith took a deliberately big sip before answering. "I have my very own bodyguard that you hired yourself. You obviously trust him. There's no reason I can't have a good time tonight." And with that, she downed the rest of her drink and placed the glass on the bar. "I think I'll find someone to dance with."

"I'll join y..." At the look on Jason's face, which he knew was furious, his mother's words trailed off. "I think I'll stay with Jack, that's what you said your name was in the car earlier, right?" she asked of the bodyguard.

"Yes, ma'am." The man didn't crack a smile. He took his job seriously.

"Do not move from here," Jason instructed his mother before heading after Faith.

She'd had a head start and was already on the dance floor and had found a willing partner. A definite Wall Street type with slicked-back hair, a white shirt, sleeves rolled up, and an arrogant look on his face, he had just reached out and put his hand on Faith's waist.

Jason thought he was going have an aneurysm. Blindly, he stepped forward, grabbed the man's arm, and swung him away. "She's with me."

The other guy narrowed his gaze, his face flush with embarrassment as he fixed his shirt, brushing out wrinkles. "Relax, man. If she's yours, keep her on a leash," he muttered and walked away, which was smart because Jason was still raging with anger that another man had touched her.

"Are you happy?" he asked Faith. "Did you get what you came for tonight?" Because no doubt she'd wanted a rise out of him after being ignored ... and he'd given her one.

A sad expression crossed her face. "Not at all, Jason. Your mother wanted to come. Once I was here, I just decided to have a good time. I haven't been out like someone my own age in over a year. It had nothing to do with you." Turning her back to him, she started for the bar.

"Faith."

She spun back.

"Like hell it had nothing to do with me." He paused, knowing they needed to have this out, even if it was in the wrong place at the wrong time. Even if people were watching. "I needed space, so sue me."

She braced her hands on her hips, her gaze narrowing. "I needed fun. So sue *me*." She took a step away.

He grasped her around her waist and flung her over his shoulder, striding back toward the private area upstairs.

"Hey! Put me down!" She smacked his back.

He merely braced a hand on her lower back and ass and walked faster, pounding up the stairs. Once he was in the joint office space, he slid her to her feet. Ignoring her outrage and yelling at him, he grabbed her hand and pulled her toward his private office.

"Where are we going?" she asked, but she was no longer fighting but rushing after him.

Desire pulsed through his veins. It had been there since he'd looked down and seen the swell of her breasts in that sexy dress. The fury he'd been feeling since she challenged him, picking up another man, burned in his veins, changing into a pulsing, beating need inside of him. Putting distance between them? Taking his space? He'd never stood a chance.

But he'd hurt her, he knew. And that had never been his intention. So if she didn't want him now, he'd let her go.

"We're going somewhere we can be alone." He paused, meeting her gaze. "Any objections?"

The seconds that passed felt like long, painful ones. She stared at him, a myriad of emotions racing across her expressive features so fast he didn't try and decipher them all. Instead he waited, his cock throbbing inside his slacks.

"Faith?" he asked because she had to agree.

"What are you waiting for?"

His hand wrapped more tightly around hers as he rushed them into his office, slammed the door, and locked it behind them. He walked her to the desk and met her gaze, pleased to see her eyes dark with yearning.

"Panties off, dress up," he instructed.

Her eyes opened wide but she didn't hesitate. She wriggled the dress up and slid her sexy underwear down and off her legs.

His fucking hand shook as he unhooked his pants and dropped them, along with his boxer briefs, to the floor. "Bend over," he said in a gruff voice.

"I–"

"Up to you." He grasped his cock and pumped

once, twice with his hand.

Her eyes followed the rough movement.

She bent over the desk.

She was gorgeous, that soft, creamy flesh calling out to him. He walked behind her and nudged her feet wider, making room for himself between her thighs.

He slid one hand through her creamy folds, finding her soaked. "Jesus, you're wet."

"For you, Jason. Only for you. But if you walk away again right after, I'm done."

Her words sliced through his chest. He pushed them aside for now, knowing he was in it until her brother was caught. In it until they called it quits at the end. She knew what he wanted … and didn't. He'd been a coward for running from her.

In response, he grabbed his cock, lined it up at her entrance, and nudged himself in, sliding inside slowly as she gripped tight around him.

He closed his eyes, letting himself feel the sensations. She wasn't able to watch his face, to see how deeply she affected him, so he allowed himself the luxury of feeling.

"Harder, Jase." She wriggled her ass and he pinched one cheek, then slammed in deep.

She screamed but it wasn't like anyone could hear. Before he could ask if she was okay, she groaned. "So good. Again."

He took a slow, torturous glide out of her clasping

walls and thrust back in. Knowing what she wanted, needed, he began a steady rhythm, one hand on her back, the other on her hip as he took her hard and fast. It didn't take long for her to rise, and the slow moans became louder and more frenzied.

"Oh, God, Jase. Don't stop. I need to come."

He had no intention of denying either one of them. His blood boiled hot in his veins, his balls were drawn up tight, and the only thing holding him back from his climax was the fact that she hadn't reached her own yet. He slid his hand around her waist and rubbed his finger over her clit.

That was all she needed. She cried out and she began to climax, her trembling, shaking orgasm triggering his release. He slammed into her over and over, and when he finally thrust one last time, he knew he was so fucking gone and lost over this woman he might never find his way back.

FAITH WAS CERTAIN her cheeks still burned with the embarrassment she'd felt returning to the club after having the most explosive sex of her life in Jason's office. She felt certain everyone looking at her *knew*. Worse, she was afraid his mother knew and she couldn't meet Savannah's gaze.

Acting as if nothing were wrong, his mother chatted with them the entire way home. Jason had sent Renault on his way. Savannah went on about how much she loved the club, how Tanner had told her all the new ideas they were planning, and how she knew it would be a success. Slowly, Faith had begun to relax, and as they entered the lobby, she felt boneless and as content as she could feel given the state of her life.

As they entered the beautiful glass and marble lobby, with a doorman in the center, Jason stopped short. Savannah gasped. And Faith looked at the tall man who was the cause of their reaction.

"Robert!" Savannah stood in shock, staring at the man who looked as if he'd been waiting for hours. His suit was rumpled, his tie undone, his shirt unbuttoned, and he appeared exhausted.

"What do you want, Dad?" Jason stepped up to the other man and asked.

Robert looked at his wife. "I want to talk."

"But Mom doesn't want to see you." Jason put himself between his parents, taking his mother's side.

Staring at the man, Faith could see where Jason got his good looks. He was a true combination of both parents, who were now at a standoff as they looked at each other. A glance at Savannah, and the longing in her face was obvious. She still loved her husband.

"This is really between me and your mother, son." Robert sent a pleading stare to his wife.

"But Mom ran here, so that makes it my business.

Now if she wanted to see you, I wouldn't get involved. But seeing as how she made it clear she wants to be left alone..." Jason let his voice trail off, his meaning obvious.

Faith really felt bad for him, a son stuck between both parents, although Jason didn't really seem torn.

"Can we do this upstairs, please?" He glanced at the doorman, who, caught watching, looked down immediately. Then his stare came to Faith, a stranger to him.

Jason pulled her close. "She's with me and she stays. You don't warrant an introduction," he muttered. "As for talking, it's up to Mom."

Savannah looked shaken but she stepped forward. "Five minutes," she said softly.

They took the elevator up in awkward silence. Jason let them into the apartment, unset the alarm, and glanced at his mother. "Should I stay or go?" he asked.

"Stay," his father said, surprising Faith. "You need to hear this, too."

"Fine." Jason's curt tone told Faith all she needed to know about his mood.

She squeezed his arm in understanding and comfort. "I'll go wait in the bedroom." She started to walk away only to find herself pulled back against his chest, his arms wrapping around her middle. "I want you here."

Then she wasn't leaving.

Chapter Nine

ONCE UPON A time, Jason had a good relationship with his father. When Jason thought Robert Dare was just *their* father, his, Alex's, and Sienna's. After their world blew apart and Robert shattered his image as a dad to look up to? Well, not so much. Jason couldn't imagine why his father wanted him in the room now. Maybe he thought he'd get support from his son. If so, Jason hoped the man wasn't holding his breath.

They settled into the family room, his mother and father on opposite sides, Robert taking the chair, his mom on the far end of the sofa away from him, with Jason pulling Faith close to him on the other side.

Why did he want to subject Faith to his father's drama? Because he needed her support and he wasn't ashamed to admit it.

Dealing with his father was draining, keeping track of his truth and lies difficult. But here they were.

Jason had no intention of making it easy on his father, so he waited in silence for the other man to speak.

Finally, Robert cleared his throat. "I want you back, Savannah. I made a mistake and I'm sorry."

Jason frowned. *Mistake* was putting it mildly. Jason might make a lot of *mistakes* over the course of his life, but cheating on a woman would never be one of them.

"We went through this," his mother said. "I'm not interested in taking you back. It's not like you cheated once and corrected your ways." Savannah leaned forward in her seat. "You burned Emma in ways I can't comprehend, and I hate myself for staying with you anyway. So you're not going to convince me you're a different man now." Her cheeks were flushed and her voice steady.

Faith eased back against him, obviously knowing it wasn't easy for him to hear his mother talk that way about herself. It hurt. But from that pain would come renewed strength. Jason was seeing it firsthand for himself.

Robert had the grace to look ashamed as he glanced at the floor before meeting Savannah's stare once more. "Look. I'm no angel, we both know this."

"That's an understatement," Jason muttered.

His father ignored the dig. "I'm a prick. I've done shitty things to Emma and the rest of my kids. I never knew how to handle the dual life. I actually felt guilty about hiding you all, and I took it out on them, not giving them the parent they deserved. I didn't love their mother, so I wasn't good to them. I can't justify it..." He trailed off, then looked down at his hands, which he was twisting together.

"Robert," she began.

He drew a deep breath, paused, then said, "Please let me finish. I love you, Savannah. I always did. I'm weak. I never admitted that before. But I want the life I have with you."

Jason glanced at his mother to find tears trickling from her eyes. Faith clasped his hand tight.

Jason blew out a long breath. If he had to say whether or not he believed his father ... the best he could say was Jason thought Robert believed his own words. Did it change anything? Did Jason trust the man to change? Hell no.

"Well? Can you find it in your heart to forgive me?" Robert asked.

Jason held his breath, and so did Faith by his side.

"No." His mother rose to her feet, her pretty silver dress sparkling and seeming too nice for this awkward moment. "You cheated on your first wife. You cheated on me. You're a no-good, worthless excuse for a man and I'm done. I'm going to like myself for a change, and for that to happen, I need to get rid of you."

Robert jumped up, surprise on his face. He'd really

thought Savannah would forgive and forget. "But–"

"No. The door is this way."

Jason and Faith remained sitting, letting his mother precede him to the door. He heard mumbling and then the door opened and slammed shut. He assumed his father was gone. Footsteps told him his mother was going directly to her room.

"Are you okay?" Faith asked softly.

He shifted in his seat so he could meet her gaze. "Yeah. This family drama? I'm becoming immune." He managed a laugh. "Or at least I've learned to distance myself from it. But I'm so damned proud of my mother."

"She is pretty awesome," Faith said, resting her head on his shoulder. "It'll be okay, you know."

He pulled her tight, breathing in her sweet scent. "Yeah." On the family stuff?

He agreed.

On life in general? That was anyone's guess.

✧ ✧ ✧

THE NEXT MORNING, Savannah, looking strong and satisfied with her decision, broke the news that Sienna had asked her to come stay with her. She didn't have a nanny, nor did she want one, though her husband could well afford it. But she did need her mother, and since Savannah was here, Sienna wanted her. And

Savannah was thrilled to help with the baby and spend time with her granddaughter.

A win-win all the way around, Faith thought, as she sat sharing her last cup of coffee with the woman she'd come to like a great deal. Savannah was warm and friendly, genuine and real.

"It's been nice getting to know you," Faith said, glancing at Jason's mother over her coffee cup.

The other woman smiled. "I feel the same way."

"You remind me of my mom," Faith said.

Savannah tipped her head to the side. "You miss her."

Faith nodded over the lump in her throat. "It's hard. And I had her necklace that she wore every day, but my brother took it when he ransacked my apartment." She wiped at a tear that fell. "Jason has his PI looking for it in pawnshops, but I've resigned myself to the fact that it's lost forever."

Which seemed to be a theme in her life. Things lost to her. Her father. Her mother. Even her brother. All gone. And one day soon, Jason would be, too.

"I like the time I spent with you. I just wanted you to know that," Faith told Savannah.

"You never know, you might end up sticking around," she said, hinting at something more happening between Faith and Jason.

Faith shook her head. "I hate to burst your bubble,

but honestly, Jason doesn't want the same things I do."

"Which are?" Savannah tucked a strand of hair behind her ear and leaned in close, waiting for her to answer.

"One day, when danger isn't lurking? I want a husband, a family. Kids," she whispered. And though she knew without a doubt she wanted those things with Jason Dare, he'd made it clear he wasn't ready. Would probably never be ready.

"Listen, honey. He went through a real life-altering tragedy. I have to believe he will come out the other side ... with the help of the right woman." Reaching out, Savannah took her hand. "I know I'm meddling but I've seen how you two look at each other. I believe you're that woman. It'll take patience ... and faith," she said, laughing at her own joke.

Faith grinned. "We'll see. But you have a lot more to worry about than Jason and me."

"Yes. Yes, I do. But I believe I've taken the right first step."

Faith smiled as Jason walked into the room. He'd been taking a shower. His hair damp, he wore a pair of jeans and a tee shirt, his standard outfit for daytime at the club. He changed there for the nighttime shift. They'd agreed to stick to the same work schedule with Renault as her bodyguard.

He really did need to be at work and she understood. Now that they'd discussed it like rational adults,
without him just pulling away, she had no problem
with the change. In fact, she was so grateful he was
going out of his way to help her like this. The only way
she could think of to repay him was to let him go
easily and the way he wanted when this nightmare with
her brother was over.

"Are you all packed to go to Sienna's?" Jason
asked his mother.

"Yes. I can't thank you enough for letting me intrude on you two."

Waving away the comment, Jason grasped his
mother's hand. "Just be happy."

Once again, Faith found herself with tears in her
eyes. This was a man capable of deep love, affection,
and understanding. If only he would extend those
same things to himself, he, too, could be what he
wanted for his mother.

Happy.

✧   ✧   ✧

A WEEK AFTER his mom moved out, Jason sensed
Faith's restlessness. She wanted her brother caught
and she wanted it yesterday. Jason sensed the man was
merely biding his time, waiting for the right moment
to strike. He probably hoped to find Faith alone,

something that wouldn't happen under Jason's watch.

Jason, on the other hand, hoped to prolong their situation as long as possible. It wasn't that he thought Faith desired to leave him; no, she just wanted her life and her freedom back. Sadly, they were both aware that came with the end of their relationship as it existed now. She would move out. She'd work days. He'd work his long hours day and night. And he'd have to let her go ... to find what he'd heard her telling his mother she wanted. A husband and kids.

Before he could delve deeper, his phone rang and he saw it was Jack Renault. "Hey. What's up?" Jason asked.

"We got a break," Renault said in his always dead-pan voice. "I'd sent out pictures of the necklace to other PIs and friends of mine and someone found it. They're going to drop it off at the club, because believe it or not? The pawnshop was right around the corner. We'd checked the place once before, so we're thinking it was pawned off more than once. Either way, it's in our hands. And we're tracking it backwards. Hope to have more soon."

Jason's heart beat harder. Faith was going to be so happy she'd have this piece of her mother back. "Thanks. That's great news."

"I love results," Renault said. "And your girl is fine. I've got eyes on her now. So everything's good.

Check in with you later." He disconnected the call.

Your girl.

The words stayed with him, even as he collected the necklace from Renault's associate and headed over to return it to Faith.

✦   ✦   ✦

FAITH HAD JUST finished a batch of strawberry lemonade truffles and placed them in the front case when the bell over the front door rang and Jason walked in. Whenever she looked at him, it was like seeing him for the first time, and that ripple inside her was just as potent.

Kelsey came out from the back to see if she could help and stepped close to Faith. "You're one lucky woman," she whispered, eyeing Jason, then returned to the kitchen in the back.

They'd just had a busy spurt and now things at the shop had died down, so she headed out from behind the counter and strode up to him. "So what brings you by?"

"Good news." His eyes sparkled with a happiness she hadn't seen there before.

"What is it?"

He grasped her elbow and led her to a set of chairs, nowhere near where Renault lingered in his own corner. The man acknowledged Jason with a tip of his head and gestured toward the door. Since Jason was here, he was obviously going outside. As much as Faith appreciated the security, she was beginning to feel smothered by people constantly being in her space.

Not Jason, though. "So are you going to tell me?" she asked.

"Look what turned up." Reaching into his pocket, he pulled something out. She noticed a flash of gold, and then he dangled a very familiar necklace in front of her.

"Oh my God!" She held out her hand and he dropped the piece into her palm. Tears welled in her eyes as she curled her hands around the cool piece of jewelry. "This means everything to me." She looked up at him in disbelief.

"I told you I'd do everything I could to get it back to you," he said in a gruff voice.

She wrapped her arms around his neck and pulled him close, breathing in his masculine scent as she hugged him tight. "Thank you."

Stepping back, she asked, "Will you put it on for me?" She didn't want to take the heart necklace off again for a long time.

"Sure."

She lifted her hair and turned, her back facing him so he could wrap the chain around her neck and hook the clasp. His big hands fumbled a little and he grunted before finally succeeding. "Got it."

She was about to release her hair when he leaned down and brushed his lips over the sensitive skin on the nape of her neck. She shivered, her nipples puckering and a sudden swell of desire rushing through her veins.

"Jason," she said softly, dipping her head.

In reply, he swept his mouth over her skin and bit down gently with his teeth.

She shivered, backing against him, feeling his hard body come into contact with hers and the ridge of his erection nudging her back. She turned, cupping his face in her hands, and kissed him, sliding her tongue into his mouth. But she was aware of where they were, and having been caught once before by a customer, she kept it brief, stepping away despite wanting so much more.

She brushed her hair out of her face and glanced at him, his eyes dark with need.

"How do you expect me to go back to work now?" he asked, not so discreetly adjusting himself.

She grinned. "At least I know you'll be thinking about me."

"I'm always thinking about you, sweetness."

She was more affected than she should be by that nickname he'd given her. "Thank you again for my necklace." She touched the heart that now lay around her neck, a reminder of the mother she loved so deeply.

"You really should be thanking Renault and company. They scoured the shops," Jason said, deferring the compliment.

She patted his cheek. "But it was your idea to hire him to look for it, so just accept my gratitude and go back to work. I need to help Kelsey in the back."

"One more thing?" he asked.

"What's up?"

He blew out a long breath and said, "We've hired the first live act for the club and they're playing a week from Friday."

"That's great! Did Grey say yes?" she asked, happy for him.

His frown took her by surprise. "I wish he had. But no. His former bandmate, Lola Corbin, is going to perform instead."

"From Tangled Royal? I love her!" Faith clapped her hands like the excited fan she was.

"She'll be singing with Charlotte Jasper," Jason said, shifting on his feet, his expression taut.

"She's a big name, too, right? So what's wrong? You seem uptight about it." She rubbed at the throbbing in his right temple, a clear indication he was bothered by this whole conversation.

"Charlotte's my ex," he said, as if bracing for an argument.

Faith narrowed her gaze. "And?" She hadn't thought he was celibate before her.

"I just don't want you to be..." He trailed off and she could only guess at what he had been about to say.

"Jealous?"

"More like uncomfortable with the idea of her being around, I guess." He shoved his hands into his pants pockets.

Faith was a lot of things, but a clinging female wasn't one of them. "If she's an ex, I don't see the problem. Unless there's still something between you?" At the thought, jealousy began to seep through her, and she didn't like the feeling.

"Not for me," Jason rushed to assure her. "It's just that she was persistent when I ended things, and I'm worried she's going to take the opportunity to perform as something more than a professional invitation."

Faith tipped her head to the side, staring at Jason. She thought about the pop performer, a gorgeous raven-haired beauty who preferred red lips to Faith's light gloss and who was much thinner than Faith with her curves. Charlotte was famous and seemed to have it all. But Jason had obviously ended their relationship, so he didn't want the other woman. He was with Faith.

Should she be jealous? Maybe. Was she? Only to the extent that any woman would be.

She and Jason had a solid relationship for what it was. She knew better than to expect a future, but she did require fidelity. Given Robert Dare's history and Jason's reaction to his father's behavior, Faith wasn't worried Jason was a cheater.

She reached out and grasped his hand. "Will you be coming home to me after she performs? If so, I don't see a problem."

He let out a relieved breath. "I just assumed you'd have issues with my ex performing. Just like I'm assuming she'll still want me when, in all probability, she's moved on. It's not like I've heard from her recently."

"You see? You're uptight for no reason." She had a dawning realization. "I know you didn't like it when I came to the club with your mother, but you have to know I'm not going to miss this performance."

He closed his eyes and groaned. "I don't want to worry about your safety while being concerned the night goes off as planned."

She shrugged. "Then leave that worry to my body-guard over there." She gestured to Renault, who'd returned to his corner. "And you worry about your business."

"I just have a bad feeling about you being in the

crowded club." He met her gaze, a plea in his expression, but she wasn't going to give in.

"As long as I'm with you and protected, I'll be safe." She kissed him on the cheek, not wanting him to worry.

She worried enough for both of them, but she refused to miss his big night.

✧   ✧   ✧

THE DAYS BEFORE Club TEN29's big concert took a lot of time and planning and kept Jason out late every night. It reached the point where he barely saw Faith, who was sleeping when he came home and gone when he woke up in the morning. Now that he was back to working normal shifts, his hours were the complete opposite of hers. But he was determined to make this shift in the club's vision all it could be, and if that meant sacrificing his personal life, so be it.

He hadn't lied to Faith when he'd told her he had an uneasy feeling something was going to go down on the night of the concert. Her brother couldn't stay hidden forever. He wouldn't, not if he wanted his money. He was going to come after her when she was vulnerable, and where would she be more susceptible than in a club loaded with people?

But he couldn't keep her prisoner, which meant she would be coming to the club. So he'd have to split his focus in order to make sure she was safe ... and he would because, when it came down to it, she meant everything to him.

Faith had slipped behind the carefully constructed walls he'd erected and become part of his family, part of his life, and integral to his well-being. He'd never have believed it could happen and yet it had. If he lost her now, he'd hurt as badly as he had when he'd lost Levi. Now that she was in, he was never letting her go.

Levi, he thought, would want him to live his life. To honor him in all ways, not dwell on the past and never climb out of the horror they'd experienced. Although he hadn't realized it before, he understood that now. Faith showed him he could have a future. Not one defined by Robert Dare's mistakes or by tragic loss.

Now he just had to get Faith's brother out of her life, and then he could tell her how he felt and hope she believed how far he'd come.

✧   ✧   ✧

IZZY CALLED FAITH and invited her to go dress shopping with Jason's sister, Sienna, for Club TEN29's big concert event. It took a lot of arguing for her to get Jason to accept the fact that she could go to department stores and boutiques and be safe. She'd had to agree to have Renault trailing her every step of the way, and she felt sorry for the big man watching three women laugh their way through trying on at least fifty dresses before even hitting the shoe department in the store.

For the first time since she'd moved to New York, she was free to do what she wanted with friends, or at least with Jason's female relatives, who felt like they could be her friends. The day brought her face-to-face with what she'd been missing in her life, and she promised herself when Colton was caught, she would build a full life for herself.

They had finished their shopping, loaded the bags into the trunk of Izzy's SUV, and were now sitting around a table in a restaurant in Midtown.

Because Sienna was breastfeeding, she had a club soda in front of her, but Izzy and Faith had mimosas. They all ordered Oriental salads, and while waiting, they talked.

"To a successful day," Sienna said, raising her alcohol-free glass.

"Hear, hear." Izzy touched her glass to Sienna's and the three of them each did the same.

"Izzy, I can't thank you enough for letting me put my business card on the table at Noah's party. I have been inundated with calls. Even moms whose kids' birthdays aren't until the summer wanted me to schedule them on my calendar."

The pretty blonde smiled and raised her glass again. "To growing your business."

"Thank you."

"So," Sienna said. "What's really going on between you and my brother? And don't tell me you're just friends." Her eyes glittered with mischief.

Faith choked on her drink. After coughing, she dabbed at her wet eyes.

"She's blunt," Izzy said needlessly. "And much younger, so we'll have to forgive her."

A twenty-three-year-old Sienna wrinkled her nose. "Hey. I have enough older brothers meddling in my life that I can do the same in theirs if I want. But I apologize if I'm being too nosey," the pretty blonde said.

Faith smiled, feeling her cheeks burn as she answered. "Oh, there's a lot going on," she admitted. "But it has an expiration date. When my brother is finally caught and we get him out of my life and I move out of Jason's apartment, we'll go our separate ways." Her stomach lurched, and though she wanted to blame the alcohol, she knew for a fact it was the thought of leaving Jason that upset her.

Sienna sighed. "My father's behavior made all of us wary of relationships, but I really hoped that Jason would find the right woman and settle down."

Faith placed her drink down on the table. "I think

it's more than just your father." She wouldn't betray any confidences Jason had given her about his past.

"Oh, I know. Losing Levi devastated him." Sienna's face crumbled, her pain for her brother clear. "All those guys were destroyed, really. But instead of shutting people out, Jason should embrace the good in life and live it to the fullest." She clearly wanted the best for her brother, but she didn't want to accept his choices.

Faith couldn't help but feel protective of Jason and his feelings, even if they weren't in Faith's best interest. "Jason really is entitled to react his own way, and if he doesn't want the kind of future I do, that's okay." She forced the words out, because in her heart, she meant them, no matter how painful the thought.

Did she want everything with the man? Hell yes. But she wouldn't force or judge his choices. "Can we talk about something else?" She didn't want to get more upset and cry when there was nothing she could do about the situation she found herself in.

"Let's talk about candy," Izzy said. "Faith is a master."

"Sure. I'm sorry," Sienna murmured. "So tell me about your business. I love sweets and I'm sorry I haven't come by before, but now that I have Mom to help out, I'm going to visit you."

"That would be lovely. How is your mom?" Faith

asked.

With a sigh, Sienna sipped her club soda before answering. "She's stronger than I knew. And she has the entire family's support, even my half siblings. Everyone's come around and embraced her. I'm so glad."

"Savannah's a sweet woman. I'm glad the family is a whole unit at last."

The waitress walked over and placed their salads in front of them, ending conversation, leaving Faith alone with her thoughts while they ate in relative silence. Instead of dragging herself through a sad rehashing of losing Jason sometime soon, she thought about the dress she'd bought for the concert. She'd gone overboard, choosing a red garment that came to above the knee and dipped low in the front with a slit up one thigh.

She'd surpassed her budget, but she had a feeling this was her final chance to make a lasting impression on Jason Dare, and she decided the splurge was worth it. He might let her go in the end but she'd give him a sexy, stunning vision to remember her by.

Chapter Ten

THE MORNING OF the big event, Jason sat with his partners in the main office, a bottle of bourbon just opened for a toast before they made their way downstairs and got to work. Despite none of them being major drinkers, a toast to their success was something to be savored. And they knew Levi would approve.

"Jason, we owe this night to you." Tanner raised a glass. "It's your idea come to life."

"And I owe it to Faith for planting the initial germ of an idea." Who would have thought the night he'd seen the sexy blonde on the side of the road would have changed his life as much as it had?

Landon placed his glass on the counter and met Jason's gaze. "Sounds like she's special."

"She is." Jason took a drink of the only alcohol he'd allow himself tonight. "More than I ever thought possible."

Tanner shifted on his feet. "More power to you, buddy. But that's not for me."

"Me, neither," Landon muttered. "I can't see anyone ever changing my way of thinking. I'm good on my own."

Jason frowned. "You don't know what you're missing. But I know there's no convincing you unless you experience the power of it for yourself."

Tanner rolled his eyes at that. "Love is not for me. No one's going to understand me or accept the demons inside me. Except you two." He smirked as if it didn't bother him.

Except Jason sensed it did. But he wasn't going to argue with the man. Only the right woman coming along would change his way of thinking.

"Okay, so for tonight … is security tight?" Jason asked.

Tanner nodded. "Nothing to worry about on that score. I've got everything locked down."

Jason blew out a breath. "And I've got a bodyguard on Faith. Which means I guess we've done all we can."

Landon nodded. "I suggest we try to enjoy, too. The talent is downstairs. Lola and Charlotte are doing sound checks."

Jason sat on the corner of the desk, "Yeah. I ran into them on my way up here." And he'd wiped Charlotte's red lipstick marks off his lips soon after. If she'd gotten over him the way he'd hoped, she had a funny way of showing it. Then again, Charlotte liked to be the center of attention and to cause drama. Hopefully that's all her big hello was all about.

"I need to change my clothes. I'll meet you guys downstairs," Jason said.

Landon glanced down at his jeans. "I think we all need to dress." With the amount of hours they spent at this place, it was their second home, and they chose to be comfortable until it was time to head down to the floor.

"Are you going home to pick up Faith?" Tanner asked, rising to his feet from the chair he'd been sprawled in.

Jason shook his head. "Renault, the bodyguard, is bringing her. Apparently she wanted to get her hair and makeup done with some of the women in my family."

A dark chuckle came from Tanner's throat. "You're in trouble, man. When the family gets involved, it's harder to end things."

Jason grinned. "That's the point, my friend. That's the point."

✧   ✧   ✧

FAITH'S HEART BEAT with excitement as she traveled with Jack Renault to Club TEN29. She'd had a fantastical day with Izzy and Sienna, from having her hair done professionally to visiting with a makeup artist, who made Faith look incredible. She couldn't remember the last time she'd felt so good about herself. So full of energy to go out, forget her problems, and have fun.

She didn't even care that she'd put an excessive amount of money on her credit card to make tonight happen. This was a big night for Jason, and it might be the only night they spent together dressed up and enjoying his success. Pushing aside those thoughts, she glanced out the car window in time to see the club.

They were here.

She allowed her bodyguard to escort her inside, past the line that wrapped around the corner, then looked around for someone she knew. She expected Jason to be busy and she didn't want to be underfoot. She just wanted to experience his big night along with him.

Music blared around her, the thumping of the beat reverberating inside her. She could only imagine the sound and feeling when the entertainment began to play.

Her gaze fell to the bar, where the Dare women were congregated. She joined Izzy and Gabe, who welcomed her warmly. Sienna showed up next with her mother and husband. She introduced Faith to her husband, Ethan Knight, an imposing-looking man who she wouldn't want to cross. All the men in this family were alpha to the extreme, Faith mused, thinking about how lucky the women were to have found men willing to commit.

She bit down on her cheek. She'd promised herself she wouldn't go there tonight. She wouldn't think about endings or things she couldn't have. She glanced at Savannah Dare, admiring her strength for walking away from a bad situation and not sitting at home and sulking while she pulled herself together after the way her marriage had crumbled.

Not feeling as cheeky as she had last time she was here, Faith ordered a Pinot Grigio and looked around as the club began to fill with people. Since she hadn't seen any of the partners, she assumed Jason and the other men were busy with last-minute preparations.

All the while, her big bodyguard stood nearby, the only reminder that everything in her life wasn't as perfect as it seemed at an outside glance.

She was making small talk with Jason's family when she had the distinct feeling of being watched. She glanced over her shoulder and up to the area that overlooked the expanse of the club floor. Sure enough, Jason stood on the balcony above the bar area, staring down ... at her.

She picked up her wineglass and took a sip, her gaze never leaving his, wondering if he could read her mind. If he knew how hard she'd fallen for the man who'd taken her in and looked after her when he hadn't known her at all. Who'd made her his priority and sole focus.

Did he know that she'd fallen in love with him?

She stared back at him, in his dark slacks, black shirt, and suit jacket, a dark, sexy, protector with eyes only for her. But a man who was willing to let her go. She promised herself she'd make it easy for him, and so she'd never reveal her feelings. Not in words, anyway.

She'd hold them tight to her heart, where she'd always hold him.

She blinked and he was gone, which meant he was probably making his way downstairs. She shivered in anticipation, suddenly eager to see him.

Touch him.

Kiss him.

He'd been working long hours that were opposite of hers and she'd spent many hours in his big bed alone. She didn't know how many more she'd spend in her own apartment with nothing but her memories to sustain her. After the break-in, they'd cleaned things up but she hadn't gone home. It was going to feel strange to be there with nothing but her memories of Jason to sustain her.

Without warning, a pair of strong arms slid around

her waist and she recognized the scent of his cologne. She sighed in pleasure and leaned back against him. "You look so fucking hot I couldn't take my eyes off you," he said in her ear.

She turned and found herself in his arms. "You're looking mighty fine yourself, Mr. Dare."

He grinned in reply, a naughty twinkle in his eye. "I want to take you home and devour you." His finger dipped into her cleavage, outlining the low vee of her dress.

Her nipples tightened and she rubbed her thighs together, desire for this man alive inside her.

"Would you two get a room?" Tanner muttered from beside them.

Jason chuckled. "Can't wait for it to be your turn."

"As if."

Before either man could utter another word, the sound of tapping on a microphone reverberated around the room, and Landon walked on stage. Dressed similarly to Jason in all black, he held the microphone in one hand.

"Welcome to Club TEN29." He raised his hands and a roar of applause came from the crowed. "We're thrilled to welcome you all to our grand reopening, featuring Lola Corbin Grissom, of Tangled Royal fame, and Charlotte Jasper!"

The crowd burst into applause as Landon stepped

out of the spotlight and the curtains went up, revealing the two superstar singers.

Jason slid his arms around her waist and rested his head on her shoulder. And that's how they stood together, listening to the most amazing live music ever. These two women were powerhouse talents, and Faith was thrilled for Jason that he'd gotten them to perform. Even Charlotte, who did like to stare at Jason despite the fact that he was firmly with Faith.

At least for now.

She leaned back into him and let herself enjoy the rest of the evening, celebrating in Jason and his partners' success.

✧   ✧   ✧

AFTER A TRIUMPHANT night, the patrons took their time leaving, but finally the crowds dissipated and the club felt empty. No music blared in the speakers. Lola and Charlotte's crew were disassembling their equipment. The cleanup team worked, sanitizing tables, then putting the chairs up high on the tables so the floors could be cleaned.

In the meantime, family and close friends huddled around the bar, still on a high. Once they were alone with vetted people, Jason sent Renault home. He'd take Faith with him. Right now, everyone around them only wanted the best for each other. For the first time in a long time, Jason, too, was soaring from the perfection of the night.

He slung an arm around Faith's shoulders. "You know I have you to thank for tonight's events."

She glanced up at him, confusion on her pretty face. "How? I don't recall coming up with the idea to turn this into a live venue for high-end performers."

"No, but you did inspire me the night we met when you talked about standing out in your own space."

"I was delivering little baskets to neighborhood businesses, not making a statement in the Manhattan nightclub world." She waved away his comment as if it meant nothing.

"Don't do that. Don't belittle what you do. Candy makes people happy."

She smiled. "I love what I do. I'm just saying how could I have inspired this awesome night?"

"You made me think bigger. Made me ask how I could make my business stand out. And the idea came to me. So I have you to thank." He pressed a kiss to her lips.

"Well, you're welcome. Who knew that my niche would end up being party favors?" she mused, but she sounded pleased with the notion.

"Like I said, you make people happy. You do, Faith."

She tipped her head to the side. "And on that note, I'm going to excuse myself and go to the ladies' room."

"I'll be waiting."

She slipped from beneath his arm and walked away. He couldn't tear his gaze from the dip of material that exposed her back, the sway of those sexy hips, or the way her hair bounced against her back as she moved.

"Jason! You're finally alone!" Charlotte came up to him, pulling him into a hug. "Thank you for letting me perform tonight. I love live audiences in small venues."

He extricated himself from her grasp. "Well, you and Lola make a dynamic team."

She smiled at the compliment. "I'm trying to convince her we should record a song together."

"I expect it would be a hit."

"So…" She flipped her hair over her shoulder, her gaze steady on his. "You looked quite … domesticated with your girlfriend."

"So what?" he asked, knowing both the description of his relationship and the fact that Faith was his girlfriend were true.

Here he was, celebrating his biggest success, and he'd wanted her by his side. Brought her to live with him. Introduced her to his family. Made her a part of his life, all the while proclaiming he didn't want anything serious.

He'd been such a dense asshole, but he had his head on straight now.

"So I thought you didn't do serious." Charlotte set her hands on her hips, clearly wanting an answer.

Jason wasn't surprised Charlotte wanted to discuss his relationship with Faith. At a glance, it was obvious what he had with Faith was deeper than anything he'd shared with the beautiful raven-haired beauty in front of him now. She might be gorgeous, but she didn't do it for him the way Faith did, and what he and Charlotte had shared? It had been fun but superficial, like all his prior relationships.

He'd always thought she'd been on the same page, as she'd been busy building her career and traveling. Until he'd broken up with her and then she'd cried like they'd been engaged or something. Yet he prided himself on always being honest with the women in his life, Charlotte included.

"Look, people change. Circumstances change." He'd met the right woman by chance on the side of the road, and his entire life had spun upside down.

She stared at him, hurt in her expression, something he'd never ever intended to do to her.

He shoved his hands into the pockets of his pants. "I'm sorry. But I was honest. I never lied to you."

"Except about what you were capable of giving."

The truth was he hadn't known what he was capable of until he met Faith. He rolled his shoulders. "When you meet the right person, you know." He pulled a deep breath. "Thank you for performing tonight and I wish you the best," he said, wanting to end this conversation.

"Right. You, too," she begrudgingly said.

Because there was nothing more to say, he turned and came face-to-face with Tanner. "Hey," Jason said.

"Hey." Tanner grinned. "*We* did it."

Jason nodded. "That we did. I–" Before he could get the next word out, the sound of a piercing scream echoed throughout the room, and his stomach plummeted because he recognized the person behind the sound.

"Faith. She went to the bathroom," Jason said, his heart pounding hard in his chest. He'd sent Renault home because the only people left were family, friends, and workers who'd been vetted. Because he'd had her back, the way he had for the last couple of months.

The hallway with the restrooms had an entry on either side of an island-like wall. "I'm going that way." He pointed to the nearest way to the ladies' room hall. "You take the back. Call 911," he yelled out to everyone who was suddenly panicking.

Tanner nodded and they took off at a run.

✦　✦　✦

FAITH WASHED HER hands in the sink, then fixed her makeup, cleaning the dark smudges from beneath her eyes and freshening her lipstick. Her feet hurt in her shoes. She didn't know how much longer Jason needed to stay, but she was more than ready to go home.

With a last look in the mirror, she strode out of the powder room and walked right into a wiry male body she recognized immediately.

"Colton." Her mouth ran dry at the sight of him. He'd never looked worse. His hair was stringy and greasy, hanging limply over his face, his eyes were glazed, and his skin tinged yellow.

"You are one hard woman to get alone."

"How did you find me to begin with?" she asked, eyeing either side of her, hoping someone would come by.

"My friend's sister works at the police station. Not that it matters. Just that I found you." He raised a shaky hand and grabbed her wrist.

She knew immediately he wasn't strong enough to hold her, and she yanked her hand away. Instead of being able to run, she teetered on her heels and twisted her foot, her ankle wrenching hard.

"You bitch." He swung his hand, slapping her hard

across the face. She'd never been hit before, and the move dazed her for a precious second, and in that instant, he reached into his pocket and pulled out a pocketknife, releasing the blade.

Needing to get someone's attention, Faith screamed, because even if Colton wasn't strong and able-bodied, he certainly was deranged and determined.

"Shut up, bitch. You've been nothing but a pain in the ass," he said as he roughly yanked her to him, pulling her up against his thin body, the his body odor overpowering.

He raised the knife to her neck. "I just want my money. We're going somewhere for the night, and first thing tomorrow, you're going to the bank and giving me what's mine. Understand?"

Careful not to move and cause him to stab her with the knife, she said, "Yes," in a deliberately tiny voice.

Although Colton's blade was small, it was sharp and she'd already felt it prick her skin. She was more afraid he'd hit an artery than she was of him in general. He was a shaking, pathetic mess of the man he'd been, but his tremors made him dangerous.

How did he think he was getting her out of here, she wondered, what with the front of the bar bustling with help and Jason's family milling around? But she didn't want to freak him out and cause him to react by asking him about that, so she voiced the other question on her mind. "How did you get inside?"

"I walked in with a huge party that was on the list." He spoke like he was proud of himself. "Then I hid in the back and hoped I could get you alone." His hand shook, which made her nervous.

She wondered when he'd had his last fix. "Colton—"

"Faith." Jason called her name as he stepped cautiously into the hallway.

She was so grateful to see him, her knees almost buckled as she met his gaze.

"You okay, sweetness?" he asked.

"Yeah." She swallowed, careful not to move.

"If you want her to stay okay, move aside and let us through." Colton nudged her forward one step. Her ankle buckled and she yelped in pain.

Jason's gaze narrowed, his fury at her being hurt obvious. "It's crowded out front," he said through clenched teeth. "Why don't you take her out the back door."

Colton shook his head. "That door's got an emergency alarm. What do you think, I'm stupid? I checked it out earlier," he said, tightening his grip.

Jason took a step forward as he spoke. "That's okay. Tanner's going to throw you out the back, aren't you, Tanner?"

It was obvious they had company, and Colton clearly realized the same thing. "Fuck!" he yelled, and whirled around to check behind him.

Jason lunged forward, pulling Faith out of his grasp and into his arms just as Tanner dove for Colton, easily taking him down, Colton's frail body no match for Tanner's more muscular frame.

"Jesus Christ." Jason lifted her face to his, running his hand gently over her cheek. "Does it hurt?"

She shook her head. "Not as much as my ankle. I wrenched it when I tried to get away." She sat back on her butt and stretched out her leg.

He gently looked at the area, holding her foot, which seemed to be swelling, in his hand. "I'm sure you just sprained it in those damned heels."

He glanced at Tanner, who had subdued her brother easily while waiting for the cops. "I was going to remind Tanner not to beat the shit out of him, but if the bastard gives him a hard time, I'm not saying a damn word," Jason muttered, then turned his gaze back to Faith.

Acting on impulse, she scrambled forward and threw her arms around his neck, holding on tight. "Thank you." Trembling, she felt better when he wrapped his strong arms around her and didn't let go.

"I hated seeing him touch you. And that knife." Jason uttered a curse. "It was small, but if it'd slipped

214

because he was shaking so hard…" He buried his face in her neck, his breath warm against her skin.

"It's over," she said, tears finally coming to her eyes. "It's all over." So much more than she was ready for.

Pulling away, Jason met her gaze. "Faith, I—"

Before he could say what was on his mind, the police rushed into the hallway, separating Jason from Faith and taking over from where Tanner all but sat on the yelling, shaking Colton.

JASON PACED THE kitchen in his apartment, his head pounding, his heart a mess. First the police had questioned them for hours, taking statements about what had transpired in the club. Faith's history with her brother took forever to explain, but, in addition to tonight's attempted kidnapping, the incidents she'd documented with the Manhattan police, plus the information she'd told the on-scene cops that her lawyer had on Colton – photographs of her bruised neck, the judge's willingness to seal her name change to prevent her from being found – meant things looked bad for her pathetic excuse for a sibling.

After calming all of Jason's family down, seeing them out, escorting Charlotte and Lola to their limousines safely, Jason left Tanner and Landon to handle closing up the club. Given the swelling of Faith's ankle, Jason had wanted to stop at the emergency room, but they'd agreed it wasn't worth the hours they'd sit waiting to be seen.

He wanted to ice it, but she'd insisted she needed a shower, wanting to rid herself of Colton's stench, and Jason couldn't deny her. He'd given her the time alone she'd requested, knowing she needed to come to terms with what had happened with her sibling.

Hell, he'd give her anything she wanted from now until the end of time. Although he'd already put his past behind him enough to move on, he hadn't realized just how much he loved her until the second he'd heard her scream. Coming around the corner and seeing Colton holding a knife to her throat had shocked him into complete acceptance.

He loved her completely and absolutely.

If anything happened to her, if he lost her, he wouldn't want to go on. Why in God's name had he believed what they had was short term and meant to end? She was a part of him and he didn't want to let her go.

He picked up the ice he'd put into a zipped bag and headed back into the bedroom only to find her wearing a pair of sweat pants and a shirt, hobbling between his closet and the suitcase she'd opened on the bed. The ice in his hands spread through his veins.

"What are you doing?" he asked as he placed the bag of ice onto the dresser by the bed.

She turned her head and met his gaze, her green eyes sad. "We agreed when Colton was caught, our time together would come to an end. I'm not going to stay here and prolong the inevitable." She ran her tongue over her lips and he wanted nothing more but to kiss her, but they needed to talk first.

"Faith—"

"Wait." She placed a stack of work tee shirts into the luggage. "I need to tell you something first. I want you to know that this isn't what *I* want."

Thank God for that, he thought, but she continued talking.

"If it were up to me, we'd stay together and see where things led. But you made it clear we had an expiration date, and because I love you, I'm giving you what you want."

Jesus, his head was spinning. Even if he had thought things between them should end – eventually – he'd never have wanted her to leave so quickly. But at this point, he didn't want her go at all.

"Let me get this straight. You love me but you're leaving," he said, summarizing her words, his heart thumping hard in his chest at the words she'd so casually tossed out. But he'd get to *that* later.

She blinked. "Yes. Because it's what you want."

217

"No." He strode over, zipped up the suitcase, and threw it onto the floor.

"Jason!"

"You're not going anywhere. First, you're going to lay that cute ass down and ice that ankle because I can see it swelling more with every minute you stand on it."

She narrowed her gaze at his rude command but it worked. She sat on the mattress and stretched out her legs. "Give it to me," she muttered, opening her hand for the ice pack.

He handed her the bag and she gingerly placed it on her swollen ankle.

"My ass isn't cute," she said under her breath.

"You're right. It isn't. It's sexy as hell. Now where were we? Right. You leaving because of what you think I want."

She wrinkled her nose at him. "What you said you wanted."

He settled beside her on the bed, easing his ass next to her thigh, forcing her to move over and make room for him to sit. "I was wrong."

Her eyes opened wide.

"You'd better savor those words, because I can't promise you'll ever hear them again."

She coughed, clearly covering a laugh. "Wrong about what, exactly?"

He leaned close, cupping her face in his hand. "Wrong to think that if I ended things with you, it would be easier. Tonight, even before Colton grabbed you, I realized that I love you."

She gasped. "You do?"

He placed his fingers over her lips. "My turn, remember?"

She nodded and leaned into him. "Go on."

"I discovered that what we shared, living together, spending hours together and not getting on each other's nerves, counting on each other, was special. It was the very thing I'd been running away from most of my life. And the only reason I was able to accept that Levi would want me to live my life, that I could open myself up to love, was because I found you."

"You love me?" she asked, her shock so real it hurt him to hear.

"Yeah. And I'm seeing that I've done a pretty shitty job of showing you."

She shook her head. "No. You've shown me every day. It's just that you were so sure you didn't want the same things that I do, and I need to know we're on the same page."

He narrowed his gaze. "How so?"

"I want it all, Jason. A house, babies, a dog, my job, your job, us coming home to each other at the end of the day. But you said you don't want kids.

And…"

"Shit," he said more to himself than to her.

"What?"

He drew a deep breath. "I was wrong. Again." To his surprise, he could look down the road and see all those things his family had, and he desired them for himself. "I want it all, too. I want kids, sweetness. And a house. I'll even take a white picket fence, as long as it's with you."

A tear fell from her eye and he wiped it away with his finger. "I never want you to cry because of me."

"It's relief. When I pulled out that suitcase, I really thought I was leaving. I promised myself I wasn't going to tell you how I felt, that I would make it easy for you, but I couldn't go without you knowing how much I love you."

"You're brave and strong … and you're mine." He picked up the ice pack and placed it onto the nightstand. "Now I'm going to make love to you and show you how I seal the deal."

He slowly and carefully stripped her of her clothes until she lay naked on the bed, her damp hair a golden halo around her head. She watched him with wide eyes as he undressed himself, her gaze coming to rest on his thick, straining cock.

Coming over her, he didn't waste any time. He slid a finger through her slick sex, and finding her wet for him, he positioned himself at her entrance.

"I just need to be inside you." Foreplay could wait for another time. "I just want to make you mine."

She chuckled beneath him. "Silly man. I've always been yours," she said as he began to slide himself into her.

Her tight walls spasmed around him and he groaned, thrusting all the way home, until he was as deep as he could get, until they were as close as they could possibly be.

And when he began to move, rocking into her, taking her slowly, he felt every slick glide and every flutter of her sweet pussy. He wasn't going to last. It was going to be the quickest yet most intense orgasm of his life. And he was taking her along for the ride.

He came at the same time she cried out his name, and the emotions that swept through him were potent. Because he was with the woman he loved and he'd finally opened himself to believe in forever.

Epilogue

THE DARES KNEW how to throw a party, Tanner Grayson thought, as he loosened the bow tie now that the wedding of his best friend and partner Jason Dare was over.

He'd never seen so many *siblings* in one place before. Being close with Jason since college, Tanner had been introduced to the many factions of the family. The New York Dares mingled with the Florida Dares; the Florida Dares no longer separated themselves by who their mother was. Glancing around, he had to admit that despite the designation of half brother or half sister or cousin, they'd become a tight-knit unit.

The only unit Tanner had was with his best friends and partners, Jason and Landon Bennett. Ever since Landon's twin, Levi, died in a hazing incident they'd been unable to prevent, Tanner had lost his ability, what little he'd had, to trust others. And despite his years-long relationship with Jason and Landon, Tanner always felt like the outsider.

The troublemaker. The one who grew up as a

have-not, unlike his friends, who, despite their emotional drama or problems, had financial stability and a close family throughout their lives. This gathering was proof of what Tanner lacked.

As they celebrated Jason and Faith's wedding, Tanner stood with Landon, neither one of them with a date, both happy to keep to themselves.

"I have to admit I never thought Jason would settle down," Landon said, tipping his head toward the man under discussion, who held his bride close as they danced.

"Agreed. But the minute he met Faith, he opened himself up to her." Tanner didn't want to allow anyone to pry him open. He might be a hothead, he might have a rough past, but he knew who he was and he knew better than to think a woman would accept him as is.

"Some would say love changes you for the better." Landon shrugged and picked up the glass of soda he drank. None of the men overindulged in alcohol anymore. Not since Levi.

"And some would say love stinks." Tanner chuckled at his own joke. "Now sex, on the other hand, that's where it's at."

Jason joined them just as Tanner made his proclamation. "Really? That's what you learned from me and Faith?"

"I learned not to pick up women on the side of the road," Tanner said, grinning at his friend. He really was happy for Jason, even if the man's future wasn't something Tanner wanted for himself. "Congratulations," he said seriously. "I wish you and Faith all the best."

"Same," Landon said.

Jason nodded his appreciation. "And I wish you two would find the right women to fill that empty hole you carry inside you."

"Not happening," Landon said.

"Agreed." Tanner had his two best friends and himself to rely on. He didn't need anything more. Or anyone.

Can't get enough Sexy? **TWICE AS SEXY** is up next.

He's the bad boy her mother warned her about.

The guy who makes her crave all the naughty things a good girl shouldn't want.

Tanner Grayson is a man outrunning the demons of his past and has the rap sheet to prove it. The only thing keeping old anger in check and him on the straight and narrow are the men he calls brothers and the club he calls home. He has no business taking the sexy woman doing shots in his club upstairs to his bed.

They never should have crossed paths. But when Assistant District Attorney Scarlett Davis lays eyes on the hot as sin club owner, she decides he's the birthday present she wants to unwrap at the end of the evening.

He tells himself it's one night. She convinces herself she deserves a short break from her latest case.

But one night isn't enough and soon these two opposites are in deeper than they ever planned.

When Scarlett's case collides with Tanner's past, she sees the dangerous man he's hidden beneath the cool veneer he presents to the world. Can she accept him for who he is? Or will she run from the bad boy who makes her feel so good?

GET **TWICE AS SEXY!**

Want even more Carly books?
CARLY'S BOOKLIST by Series – visit:
http://smarturl.it/CarlyBooklist

Sign up for Carly's Newsletter:
http://smarturl.it/carlynews

Carly on Facebook:
facebook.com/CarlyPhillipsFanPage

Carly on Instagram:
instagram.com/carlyphillips

About the Author

Carly Phillips is the *N.Y. Times* and *USA Today* Best-selling Author of over 50 sexy contemporary romance novels featuring hot men, strong women and the emotionally compelling stories her readers have come to expect and love. Carly's career spans over a decade and a half with various New York publishing houses, and she is now an Indie author who runs her own business and loves every exciting minute of her publishing journey. Carly is happily married to her college sweetheart, the mother of two nearly adult daughters and three crazy dogs (two wheaten terriers and one mutant Havanese) who star on her Facebook Fan Page and website. Carly loves social media and is always around to interact with her readers. You can find out more about Carly at www.carlyphillips.com.

3-4-20
1-24-22
1
0

CPSIA information can be obtained
at www.ICGtesting.com
Printed in the USA
LVHW082206240120
644730LV00016B/388